Lost in the darkness . . .

There was a single ringing peal, like the sounding of a vast bell from somewhere deep in the earth. Moving as smoothly as dancers in some immense demented chorus line, the robed figures turned toward Scott and Chloe. Then, without a flicker, the bonfire was extinguished and the cavern was plunged into absolute darkness.

Scott opened his mouth to shout. He wanted to tell Chloe to run. He wanted to say that going back to the home wouldn't be so bad. He wanted to run himself. But he could force no more than a tight, terrified whisper of breath past his lips, and his legs were as frozen as the stone walls.

A whispery, soft sound of movement fluttered all around them, and the rough cloth of a robe brushed past Scott's face. Chloe's grip on his fingers tightened.

"Scott!" she cried. "What—" Her voice cut off abruptly.

With wrenching force Chloe's hand was pulled away from his own.

For orders other than by individual consumers, Pocket Books grants a discount on the purchase of **10 or more** copies of single titles for special markets or premium use. For further details, please write to the Vice-President of Special Markets, Pocket Books, 1633 Broadway, New York, NY 10019-6785, 8th Floor.

For information on how individual consumers can place orders, please write to Mail Order Department, Simon & Schuster Inc., 200 Old Tappan Road, Old Tappan, NJ 07675.

E⋆TREME ZONE™

LOST
SOUL

M.C. SUMNER

AN ARCHWAY PAPERBACK
Published by POCKET BOOKS
New York London Toronto Sydney Tokyo Singapore

AN ARCHWAY PAPERBACK *Original*

An Archway Paperback published by
POCKET BOOKS, a division of Simon & Schuster Inc.
1230 Avenue of the Americas, New York, NY 10020

Produced by Daniel Weiss Associates, Inc., New York

ISBN: 0-671-01413-7

First Archway Paperback printing December 1997

10 9 8 7 6 5 4 3 2 1

AN ARCHWAY PAPERBACK and colophon are
registered trademarks of Simon & Schuster Inc.

EXTREME ZONE and the EXTREME ZONE logo are
trademarks of Daniel Weiss Associates, Inc.

Printed in the U.S.A.

IL 7+

Scott Handleson lifted his head from the thin feather pillow and looked down the long row of beds. Pale silver moonlight shone through the narrow windows of the boys' dormitory, casting bars of light and shadow through the room. The alternating stripes of light and darkness made it hard to see clearly, but as far as Scott could tell, the other boys in the Benevolence Home for Orphaned Children were solidly asleep.

At the far end of the room the single clock glowed with a faint orange light. Squinting, Scott could just make out the numbers. 11:50. He smiled in the darkness, but his heart beat with a hard, fearful rhythm. Only ten minutes to go—ten minutes before he would leave the home forever.

The whole idea of leaving the home filled Scott with a kind of terrified wonder. The real name of the place was The Children's Assistance Center and Residential Home of the Benevolent Order. Most people called it simply the Benevolent Home. For the children who lived there, the place was "Old Benny" or just "the home." Whatever it was called, Scott had been in the home since he was four years old. The small, cramped classrooms, bare dormitories, gloomy chapel, and dusty corridors of the aging buildings were his world. He had been outside, of course, but never without someone from the school along as a guardian. Even at thirteen the very idea of passing beyond the high stone walls that surrounded the play area seemed as exotic as an astronaut flying to the moon.

Scott drew in a deep breath and tried to remember the details of the plan. The air in the dorm room was filled with the soft regular sound of breathing and the occasional groan of old, worn-out bedsprings. Next to Scott one of the younger boys turned over in his sleep and muttered a stream of words under his breath. From what Scott could hear, it sounded like something from a nightmare. That didn't surprise him. There weren't a lot of pleasant dreams in an orphanage.

He heard a loud click from the far end of the room. Scott dropped back quickly to his pillow and squeezed his eyes closed as the dormitory door squeaked open. Heavy footsteps crossed the room. He dared to open his eyelids—just a crack—and saw the lean, broad-shouldered attendant named Gunter Rhinehardt marching down the central aisle. Scott quickly shut his eyes again. If he was caught now, there would be no chance to carry out the plan.

The attendant paced the length of the room, stopped, then began walking slowly back. Scott had a moment of terror as the man paused at the foot of his bed, but then the heavy footsteps started again, and the man continued on his way to the only door. There was another soft squeal of hinges as the door swung closed, then a solid clank of metal as the lock was shoved into place.

Moments later Scott was up and out of bed. He peeled off his pajamas to reveal the blue shirt and dark blue pants worn by every boy at the home. Working quickly, he arranged the pillow, the pajamas, and the blankets to make it appear that the bed was still occupied. Scott didn't believe for a second that the bed would fool anyone if the lights were turned on, but by the time the lights came on in Old Benny, he planned to be a hundred miles away.

He knelt down and dragged a small satchel from the narrow space under the bed. The bag contained everything that Scott owned, but it was still light enough to carry with one hand. He straightened, gave one last look at the bed he had slept in for as long as he could remember, then hurried toward the door.

The lock on the door was designed especially to thwart the lock-picking skills of a hundred twelve-year-old boys, and it had served that purpose well for decades, but Scott had worked hard to get past the device. With parts taken from the inside of a ballpoint pen, a flat-blade knife from the cafeteria, and a carefully whittled stick, Scott attacked the mechanism of the lock. He had practiced a hundred times when no one was looking, and he had gotten skilled enough to open the lock in ten seconds flat, but now that it was time for the real thing, Scott found his hands trembling and his fingers sweating. Twice he dropped one of his tools on the floor and had to search for them in the dark, and once he thought the whole apparatus was simply stuck. Finally he heard a rewarding click.

Scott grabbed the doorknob and turned it slowly. The hallway outside was dark and quiet. Rhinehardt and the other attendants were apparently somewhere else, making their rounds of the huge orphanage. He shut the door, carefully relocked it, and hurried down the hallway with his satchel clutched in one hand.

The arched hallways of the orphanage were dim and silent as Scott tiptoed as fast as he could toward the back of the rambling old building. His own footsteps sounded horribly loud against the old tile floors, but the farther he went, the more confident Scott felt. He was moving away from the offices and rooms at the front of the orphanage toward the abandoned, empty spaces at the rear. At this time of night no one should be nearby.

A small form suddenly detached itself from the shadows, and a hand reached out for Scott's arm. "Halt!" called a stern voice. "Who goes there?"

For a moment Scott felt swamped by a feeling of panic. Then he saw Chloe Adair's face in the shadows. "Watch it," he gasped. "You almost gave me a heart attack."

Chloe laughed. "If you're going to have a heart attack now, we might as well go back to bed. You're bound to run into things out in the real world that are scarier than me."

Scott couldn't help but smile back at her. "I don't know," he said. "You can be pretty scary."

Chloe's grin widened until it spread across her face. "Don't you forget it." A blond curl tumbled down across her forehead. Like all the other girls at the Benevolence Home, Chloe was required to keep her hair cut off at chin length. But Chloe's hair refused to cooperate with the home's idea of being neat and tidy. Like Chloe herself, her hair seemed rebellious and free spirited, always ready to drift around her head in a tangled cloud or spill down to shadow her wide blue eyes.

Scott glanced down the dark hallway ahead. "Are you sure we should go this way?" he asked. "Maybe we could just sneak out the side door."

"And maybe we could just sneak right through Father Remu's office," Chloe replied with an edge of sarcasm. "Come on, we've been planning this for weeks. The tunnel is our best way out of here."

"But we don't even know where it goes," Scott protested.

Chloe's smile turned into a look of determination. "We know it goes out of here," she said. She retrieved a small, battered suitcase from the shadows. Then she turned on her heel and walked quickly into the darkness.

Scott took a deep breath and followed her.

It had always been that way—Chloe leading and Scott following behind. Chloe was a year younger, but she had so much energy, so much focus, that she was always the leader in their games. She could be in the middle of a thousand people and she would still be the center of attention. Scott had always been a little shy. Left to himself, he probably would have stayed in the home's small library, reading the days away. But Chloe didn't leave him alone. For reasons Scott had never understood, Chloe had picked him out of all the other kids at the home. Since the ages of five and six, they had been inseparable.

For years they had played together, talked together, and studied together. And always they had gotten in trouble together. The strict rules and tight discipline of the home seemed to strangle Chloe. Every daydream she had seemed to start with escaping Old Benny and flying away into the night.

Once they had schemed to sneak out of the home by hiding in the laundry truck, but that escape attempt had been discovered before they made it past the stone walls. On a more successful day they had even managed to get into the trunk of Father Remu's own car and had been miles away before discovery. But they had been found when they tried to sneak out of the car and swiftly returned to their starting point.

After that excursion Scott had taken a beating that had left him unable to sit for three days and had been forced to stand on his chair and recite poetry instead of eating lunch. For Scott the idea of trying to escape began to seem a lot less attractive.

No punishment could stop Chloe. Within days of their capture she had proposed the plan of escaping Old Benny through the access tunnel that ran beneath the north wing. Scott had resisted. It wasn't just the fear of punishment that bothered him. Even though he was excited about the idea of escaping the dreary home, the dour people who ran it, and the hundreds of rules,

Scott was more than a little nervous about what waited for them outside. Chloe said they would be all right, but he wasn't quite convinced. He had held out for weeks, but in the end Chloe had won the argument. She always did.

The hallway ended at a flight of stairs. Chloe started down, her blond hair turning coal black as the last traces of light faded slowly away. Scott followed her into the inky depths.

The staircase was long and narrow. It curved slightly to the right as it curled downward. Though his eyes hadn't adjusted enough to see, Scott could feel the difference as the steps under his feet changed from tiles to well-worn stone, and he could smell the odor of damp clay in the air.

Chloe stopped abruptly, and Scott bumped into her. "Careful," she warned. "I'm at the door."

Scott lowered his satchel to the ground and felt ahead of him. His fingers touched old, rough wood and plates of cold, dented brass. He felt along the side of the door and brought his hand down until he found the handle, then he bent and slowly pulled his lock-picking tools from his pocket.

"How long will this take?" asked Chloe. She leaned in close beside him.

In the darkness Scott couldn't see her, but he could feel Chloe's curly hair brushing against his cheek and feel her warm breath. "It shouldn't be long," he replied. "This door is easier than the one in the dorm."

From high above there came a distant shout, followed

by the scuffle of running feet. A light switched on in the hallway, sending a column of pale yellow illumination down the curving stair.

"Uh-oh." Scott felt his heart jump as he squinted up toward the source of the light. "Looks like they noticed we were gone."

Chloe tilted her head to the side. If the idea that they were being chased upset her, Scott couldn't hear it in her calm voice. "I think they're moving away from us," she said. "They don't know where we are, and they're too stupid to figure it out anytime soon." She turned back to the door. "Get us out of this hole before someone gets lucky and wanders down here."

"Right." Scott inserted the carefully carved wooden tool into the eyehole of the immense old lock, made a careful turn to the left, and was rewarded with a loud, satisfying click. "There," he said. "That should do it."

Before either of them could move, the door swung open. Despite the light shining into the stairwell, the space beyond the door was as black and empty as a bottomless pit. Cold, damp air issued from the open door, bringing with it a smell of mold and decay.

Fresh fear crept over Scott as he stared into the darkness. Father Remu had warned all the children to stay away from the old service tunnel. Looking into the yawning blackness, Scott felt ready to obey that warning. "What if it doesn't go out at all?" he said. "What if it just goes down forever?"

"That's silly." Even Chloe's normally confident voice sounded a little shaky. She stepped past Scott and leaned through the opening. "It's fine," she said. "It'll be fine." Scott wondered if she really believed that or if she was only saying the words to try and convince herself.

From above them the sound of running and shouting drew nearer. "They must be back here," said a voice that Scott recognized as Rhinehardt's.

Scott glanced up at the light, then into the darkness behind the door. "Let's go up," he suggested. "The only thing they can do is yell at us and put us in detention. We can think of a new plan. We can—"

His words broke off as Chloe turned to face him. The shaft of light streaming down the stairway caught her face, touched her hair with warmth, and glittered in her blue eyes. For a moment Scott had a vision of the angels that decorated the home's chapel. Chloe seemed as perfect as any of them. Then he noticed that there were tears sliding slowly down her cheeks.

"I can't go back up there," said Chloe. "I don't want to be locked up anymore. All I've ever seen has been the inside of this prison. I have to get out. I have to see the world."

Scott swallowed hard. "All right," he said. "Let's go."

Chloe reached down and took his hand as they stepped together into the darkness. Scott was surprised, not just because he couldn't remember Chloe holding his hand before but at how small her fingers felt against his. With all her energy and determination, it was easy to forget that Chloe was really a very small girl. Scott had picked up six inches in the last year and was already almost as tall as some of the teachers at the home.

Chloe was a year younger and a foot shorter. Scott suddenly felt very protective of her.

The floor inside the service tunnel was smooth and damp. Scott's worn shoes slid along the ground several times, and he felt Chloe's grip tighten as she fought for her own balance. The sounds of the search in the Benevolence Home faded as they moved farther into the black tunnel, replaced by the slow distant noise of dripping water. The light dimmed until Scott could see nothing but Chloe's face floating in the darkness. Then the last of the light was gone, and he could see nothing at all. He could feel Chloe's grip on his right hand, the handle of his satchel in his left, and the damp stone under his feet. The rest of the world seemed to have vanished.

"Are you scared?" Chloe asked suddenly, her voice rising out of the darkness.

Scott thought about lying and probably would have to anyone but Chloe. "Yeah," he said. "I'm scared."

Chloe squeezed his hand. "We're out of the home. We'll find a way up soon."

"I hope so. I'm not sure I could find my way back."

"I'm never going back," Chloe replied firmly.

Scott felt his confidence rise at the tone in her voice. Even in the dark tunnel Chloe seemed as determined as ever. "All right," he said. "I just hope we get out of here before breakfast time. I've got ten whole dollars in my pocket, and I was planning on spending some of it in . . ." His words trailed away, and he slowed to a stop.

"What is it?" asked Chloe. "Is something wrong?"

"No." Scott peered ahead. "I think something's right. I think there's a light up there."

The flickering orange glow was hard to spot at first, but as they walked on, it became clearer. Gradually Scott became able to see Chloe at his side, then the walls of the tunnel became visible. For the first time he realized that they were walking in a passage with a high, curved ceiling and walls made from great blocks of dark stone. It didn't look much like a service tunnel—there were no steam pipes or electric lines, just smooth, ancient stone.

"Do you hear that?" asked Chloe.

"What?"

"Shhh!"

Scott strained to listen, but he heard nothing but the dripping water and the sound of his own breath. "What did you hear?" he whispered.

"Someone talking," Chloe whispered back, "or maybe singing."

They started forward slowly with their hands still locked together. After a dozen steps Scott began to hear the sound, too. It was a low, rushing tone, almost like water running through a vast pipe. But there almost seemed to be words to it and an irregular, jerky beat.

The yellow light was growing brighter. After another hundred feet there was enough light for Scott to see the thin gray-green layer of mold that covered the floor and the wispy tongues of fungus that hung down from the roof like some underground form of Spanish moss. The beards of white fungus swayed as they walked past, and Scott had to duck to slip under some of the longest streamers.

"We're almost there," said Chloe. Scott heard a trace of fear in her voice, but also a strange note of excitement. "Can you feel it?"

"I feel it," Scott replied. The rushing, singing, chanting sound had grown so loud, he could actually feel it vibrating through the stone under his feet, though he still couldn't make out the words. The yellow light flickered and danced over the stones around them.

Chloe tugged him forward. "Come on," she said. "Let's see what it is."

Scott's heart was hammering in his chest, and every instinct in his body told him to go back. But Chloe was pulling him on, and he had never failed to follow.

They crossed another dozen yards of empty passage. Suddenly they stepped from the tunnel into a room so vast, it was like an underground stadium. The roof soared up, vanishing into the gloom high above. The walls were at least a hundred yards apart. The stones of the walls were covered with thousands of tiny images and letters strung together in strange, spiral forms. Against the far wall Scott noticed a towering statue carved from dark, glossy red stone.

Scott had no idea what the twisted, distorted form of the statue was supposed to mean, and he had little time to look. What really drew his attention was the people.

The room was crowded with hundreds—maybe thousands—of people standing in a wide circle around a tall, crackling bonfire. All the people in the room were covered in dark robes that hid their bodies, faces, and hands. Scott had seen plenty of nuns around the Benevolence Home, and Father Remu wore a robe with a hood, but the robes worn by the people around the fire were different. Scott had the powerful feeling that these robes were meant simply to hide something terrible— that if they were to remove them, the people in the room would be as twisted and awful as the huge statue.

All at once the droning voices stopped. The vast room was filled with echoes for a few seconds and then silence. A tension filled the air that was so strong, Scott came close to screaming.

He heard a single ringing peal, like the sounding of a vast iron bell from somewhere deep in the earth. Moving as smoothly as dancers in some immense demented chorus line, the robed figures turned toward Scott and Chloe. The great bell sound came again. Then, without a flicker, the bonfire was extinguished and the cavern was plunged into absolute darkness.

Scott opened his mouth to shout. He wanted to tell Chloe to run. He wanted to say that going back to the home wouldn't be so bad. He wanted to run himself. But he could force no more than a tight, terrified whisper of breath past his lips, and his legs were as frozen as the stone walls.

A whispery, soft sound of movement fluttered all around them, and the rough cloth of a robe brushed past Scott's face. Chloe's grip on his fingers tightened.

"Scott!" she cried. "What—" Her voice cut off abruptly.

With wrenching force Chloe's hand was pulled away from his own.

At that moment Scott's frozen limbs thawed and his

13

choked throat opened. He screamed a terrible wordless yell and reached out into the darkness where Chloe had been standing a second before.

But his hands touched nothing. Nothing at all.

A beeping sound woke Scott from his doze. He sat up, rubbed his hands against his eyes, and tried to shake off the remains of the old nightmare.

He wasn't in the dark place under the earth but in a small room lit by the blue-white glow from a dozen computer monitors. He wasn't thirteen—he was eighteen. He hadn't been at the Benevolence Home in five years.

And he hadn't seen Chloe since that awful night.

Scott looked around the circle of computer screens. A million lines of text scrolled rapidly across the faces of the glowing tubes. The room rippled with light as names, addresses, birthdays, identification numbers, and a hundred other pieces of information flew past.

But the screen on the far left was still, and from the speakers beside the monitor came a steady stream of beeps. Scott spun around his chair, hoping for the best. His breath poured out in a sigh, and his chest fell.

All records sorted. No match found.

One after another the remaining machines ground to a halt, and on each of the screens the disappointing message was the same.

No match. No match. No match.

Scott lowered his face into his hands and squeezed his eyes shut. "She has to be there," he whispered with his lips against the palms of his hand.

The data he had brought back from St. Louis had held Chloe's name, but the rest of the information was encrypted in a way that left it useless. Try as he might, Scott could find no way to make sense of the files.

The door at the back of the room swung open, letting a square of light fall across the monitors. "Are you still up?" asked Kenyon Moor.

Scott turned and faced his friend for a moment. "I'm just running a few more searches," he replied.

Kenyon stifled a yawn, then shoved his hands into the pockets of his dark blue robe. "I thought you'd already searched every database in the world."

"Not quite," said Scott. "I calculated some new keys to search for."

"And I don't suppose it can wait till tomorrow?"

"No. It can't."

For a moment Kenyon only stood silently. "All right," he said. "But remember, you need to drive me to the airport in the morning."

"I'll be ready," Scott replied.

Kenyon nodded, then closed the door.

Scott turned back to the computers and entered another phrase into the search engine. One after another the screens began to fill with moving text as the programs sorted and sifted through every piece of text within their considerable reach. For a few minutes Scott sat and watched the text stream past. But it was late, and his nightmare-plagued nap had given him very little rest. Soon enough his eyelids began to droop. By the time the center screen came to a stop again, Scott was sound asleep in his chair.

This time there was no beeping from the speakers. Instead the text on the screen began to slide and flow. For a moment it appeared to be pure chaos, then a shape began to form from the letters. A nose appeared in an outline of commas and periods. A row of dashes formed a thin mouth. Parentheses marked the frames of the eyes, with a single letter *O* at their centers. More letters appeared on the screen. They filled in the face, adding shadows and highlights, until the image seemed amazingly solid.

The face began to move across the screen. The parentheses eyes blinked and turned toward the figure sitting slumped in the chair. For a moment the face was still, then the corners of the mouth changed to slashes as the dashed lips turned up in a smile. The face began to fade. The characters fell away one at a time, dissolving the features. For a moment a single line of text lingered in the center of the screen.

1 match. Target found.

Then those letters also disappeared, and the screen went dark.

ONE

Kathleen "Harley" Davisidaro backed up against a wall as a figure approached from her left. She shifted to the right, but before she had taken two steps, a door swung open as another tall form stepped into the hallway.

The muscles in her neck twisted into knots, and her hands began to tremble. She had no weapon. No way to escape.

"Harley?" a voice asked at her right elbow. "What is your *problem?*"

Harley turned and found herself looking into the round face of her friend Dee Janes. "Nothing," she said, keeping an eye on the guy walking toward her. He was skinny, with worn jeans and a T-shirt advertising a local radio station. Behind him Harley saw a cluster of younger girls enter the hall, followed by a stream of PE students dressed in shorts and T-shirts. None of them looked unusual, but Harley had to fight to hold down a feeling of panic. "There's just too many people around here."

Dee rolled her eyes. "It's a *school,*" she said with exaggerated patience. "All those people are called students and teachers. They're kind of required to be in here." She pulled open a metal locker and sifted through the disorganized contents.

"I know that," said Harley. "It's just that—"

Far down the hallway a door swung open, and a

new figure emerged from a classroom. Harley's words died in her throat, and her mouth hung open in shock.

The guy down the hallway was tall, with floppy blond hair and broad shoulders that stretched the material of his gray-and-blue Stone Harbor High School letterman's jacket. He turned and began to walk in the other direction, but even with his back turned, Harley knew who it was.

Noah Templer.

Noah. Harley moved her lips with his name, but no sound came out. Somewhere, in some part of her brain, she heard Dee calling to her, asking what was wrong, but Dee's voice seemed a million miles away. Harley stepped around her friend and started down the hall.

It seemed impossible. Noah had stepped into the glowing form that Harley knew only as the white sphere. The sphere had been generated by the secret military organization Unit 17 to act as some kind of weapon or transport. It had certainly transported Noah. He and Harley's terribly wounded father had stepped into the sphere and vanished. Since then Harley had seen her friend only in dreams. But now he was back. Somehow he had escaped the sphere. Somehow he had found his way home. Harley began to run.

Fifty yards away, Noah turned toward the doors that led into the gym. Harley pushed past a group of students, squeezed between a pair of laughing girls, and dodged around a janitor just in time to see Noah step through the door. Her science book slipped from her hands and fell to the floor, scattering papers across the hallway. Someone yelled as she bumped against her. Harley paid no attention.

She reached the gym only moments after Noah had stepped inside. Harley shoved open the door. She half expected Noah to have disappeared—like a phantom from an old story—but he was still as real as ever. He was halfway across the hardwood basketball court, walking casually toward the steps leading down to the boys' locker room.

Harley ran to catch him and reached out to touch the pebbled leather sleeve of his jacket. "Noah! How did you—"

Noah turned. And as he did, the illusion crumbled.

Harley's heart fell in her chest like a stone plunging into a well. It wasn't Noah at all. It was just another tall, blond guy in a school jacket. He didn't even look like Noah.

The guy stared at Harley with a puzzled expression. "What did you say?" he asked.

Harley stepped back. A dizzy, tired feeling swept over her, and she felt her face grow warm with embarrassment. She looked down for a moment, letting her dark hair hide her flushed cheeks. "Nothing," she replied. "I thought . . ." I thought you were my missing friend who carried my dying father into a big ball of white light and disappeared. The idea suddenly seemed so ridiculous that Harley had to fight off a hysterical laugh.

The guy in the jacket grinned. "Hey," he said. "I know you."

19

"No," Harley replied. She looked up and shook her head. "I don't think so."

"Sure." He nodded. "You sit a couple of rows over in chemistry. Your name's Kathy, right?"

It took a moment for Harley to respond. Kathleen was her own first name, and it was also the first name of the false identity she was using, but no one had called her Kathy since third grade. "Yeah," she replied at last. "Kathy Vincent."

He stepped closer and lowered his voice to a whisper. "You're the one whose dad's the big secret."

Harley nodded slowly. "I guess so."

Dee's father, the police chief of Stone Harbor, had helped arrange a cover story that allowed Harley to return to school. According to the story, Harley's father was part of the witness protection program. The cover story was supposed to be a secret, but in a town as small as Stone Harbor, Harley figured that everyone knew. The whole series of lies—the false name and the false background—made Harley very uncomfortable. She took another step back from the guy who wasn't Noah. "I need to go."

The guy in the jacket glanced around and leaned toward her. "Can I ask you something?"

"What?"

"What did your dad do?" he asked. "I heard he was in the Mafia."

Harley frowned. "No——" she began.

But the guy wasn't listening. There was an excited look in his eye. "Was your dad a paid killer? Did he knock off a bunch of people?"

"No!" Harley felt a wave of anger and disgust. "My dad never killed anyone!"

The guy in the jacket raised his hands. "Whatever you say." He backed away, still grinning. "Just don't send him to get me."

The door to the gym swung open. Harley turned and saw Dee step out onto the edge of the basketball court. "What's going on in here?" she asked.

"Just trying to stay out of cement shoes," said the guy in the jacket. With that he turned and continued on his way toward the locker room.

Harley stood there in the center of the court, feeling waves of disappointment and rage.

Dee hurried over to her side. "What are you doing in here?" she asked. "What made you start chasing Jason Edwards?"

"Who?"

"Jason Edwards," repeated Dee. She pushed back her auburn hair and nodded toward the guy. "Mr. Charming over there."

Harley turned and watched the tall figure vanish down the steps. "He's a jerk," she said firmly.

Dee laughed. "A big jerk. So why were you chasing him?"

For a moment Harley was about to explain, then she stopped and shook her head. Admitting that she thought she had seen Noah walking down the hallway sounded too crazy. "I just made a mistake. That's all."

"That's all," Dee echoed. From the tone of her voice, it was clear she was more than a little confused by

Harley's actions. She tilted her head to the side and caught her lower lip between her teeth. "Are you *sure* you're all right?"

"Yeah." Harley did her best to smile. "I'm just a little nervous, that's all."

"You've been back in school over a week now," said Dee. "When are you going to calm down?"

Harley shook her head. She turned away and watched other students passing in front of the open door to the gym. "I'm not sure I'm ever going to calm down." She swallowed hard and tried to keep her voice calm, but a raw, ragged tone crept into her words. "I don't ever feel safe. They might look like students, but any of those people out there could be an agent for Unit 17 or Umbra or Legion."

"These guys?" Dee jerked a thumb at the students streaming past. "No way. I've known just about everyone in this school since they were five years old."

"Just like you knew Josh McQuinn?"

Dee winced. "All right, give yourself ten points in the Justified Paranoia Department, but believe me—students who bleed green and dissolve into puddles of goo are definitely the exception at Stone Harbor High. Josh was one of a kind."

Harley crossed her arms. "What about Coach Rocklin?" Harley asked. "She wasn't even human."

"Oh, well." Dee shuffled through the books in her hands. "Now you're talking about the teachers. I'm not promising anything about the teachers—they're all weird." She grinned and shifted closer to Harley. "Tell

22

me, has anyone tried to kill you since you came back to school?"

"No."

"Has anyone attacked you or threatened you?"

"No."

"Has anyone sprouted antennae or grown a third arm or tried to feed you to a squid from another world?"

Harley couldn't help but grin. "No. I guess not."

Dee nodded. "Cool. See? We're just a normal bunch of kids here. Everything is going to be fine." She pulled Harley's science book from the middle of the load in her arms and held it out. "Here. I think you dropped this."

"Thanks." Harley pulled the book up against her and smiled. "Do you know how much it helps me to have you around?"

Dee raised an eyebrow. "No," she said, "but you can demonstrate your eternal gratitude and benefit yourself in the process if you will only ask Kenyon Moor to the spring dance."

Harley winced. "I'm not going to the dance."

"Why not?"

"Well, for one thing, I don't dance."

"You can learn," said Dee. "What else?"

"I don't know." Harley shrugged. "It just seems wrong to be dancing when Noah and my father are still missing."

"Noah and your dad will be back one day," Dee replied confidently. "Do you think making yourself

23

miserable is going to make them come back any faster?"

"I guess not."

"Good." Dee reached up and pressed her finger against the bridge of her nose. She had started wearing contacts weeks before and rarely put on her old glasses. But she hadn't broken the habit of trying to adjust frames that were no longer there. "What else?"

Harley pursed her lips. "I don't even know why you want me to ask Kenyon to this dance. Why do you care if either one of us goes?"

"Because," Dee explained patiently, "if you get Kenyon to go, then it'll be easier to get Scott to go." She lowered her voice. "I am a senior this year, Harley Davisidaro, and I've gone to the spring dance alone for three years in a row. This year I am going to bring a date."

Harley laughed. "All right. You win. I'll ask Kenyon."

Dee's face lit up in a huge smile. "Cool."

A bell sounded in the hallway, and the passing students increased their pace. Dee and Harley walked toward the door. "I've got to go and get bored to death in algebra," said Dee. "You want to meet after school?"

"Sure," said Harley. She looked at the crowd of students hurrying past and shivered. "I just wish I could shake this strange feeling."

"What kind of feeling?" asked Dee.

Harley shrugged. "Ever since I came back to school, I've felt like someone's watching me."

"They are," said Dee. "They're from a secret organization called 'boys,' and every one of them really is out to get you." Dee flashed a last smile, then turned and stepped into the crowd. In a moment she vanished among the taller students.

Harley stood in the doorway for a moment as the bell continued to ring. After everything that had happened, it was hard to get used to normal life, but Dee was right. If she didn't stop standing around waiting for something horrible to happen, she was going to go nuts. She took a breath, held her book against herself, and started to enter the hallway.

A hand seized Harley by the back of her shirt and jerked her roughly into the gym.

Harley spun around instantly. She shifted the heavy science book to her right hand and raised it over her head, ready to swing it like a club.

No one was there.

Harley swallowed and looked left and right. The gym was silent. "Who did that?" she called. Her words echoed through the empty space.

"I did," replied a soft voice from behind her.

Harley turned again and saw a woman in a pale blue dress standing by the door to the gym. "Who are you?"

The woman carefully closed the door and slipped the bolt home with a click. The bell outside stopped, and the sound of passing students died away. "There," she said. "Now we won't be disturbed." The woman was an inch or two shorter than Harley and very thin. The dress bared her shoulders and then dropped down in front to a level that was almost scandalous. The blue fabric of the dress matched the woman's eyes. It was a cold blue, like the ice over a deep frozen lake.

25

"Who are you?" Harley repeated. The woman didn't look particularly threatening. In fact, she looked as if she were dressed to spend a pleasant evening at a very expensive restaurant or perhaps to attend a Broadway play. But Harley knew that appearances had little to do with how dangerous a person could be.

The woman in blue leaned against the locked doors and folded her arms across her flat stomach. "My name is Abel," she said. "Lydia Abel." Her voice was soft and high, almost childish, and it held the crisp edge of a British accent. She said her name with exaggerated precision, like someone announcing the winner of a contest.

Harley shook her head. "Is that supposed to mean something to me?"

"I thought it might," said the woman. She shrugged, and her dark brown hair brushed against her bare shoulders. "I thought perhaps a mutual friend might have mentioned it to you."

Harley took a step back. The woman had made no threats, and her voice was soft and calm, but Harley felt a strange energy coming from Lydia Abel. It was like being next to a burner on a stove that had recently been turned off—the metal might look cool, but one touch would be enough to burn.

"What friend?" asked Harley.

The woman unfolded her arms. Her blue eyes fixed Harley with an intense gaze. "Ian Cain," she replied.

Harley tried to make her face as blank as possible. Agent Ian Cain had first come to her pretending to be with the FBI. Later Harley had learned that Cain was part of a much more secret organization. But even though he had lied to her about his employer, Cain had gone out of his way to help both Harley and Noah.

"I don't know anyone by that name," Harley said carefully.

"Really?" The woman laughed. Her British school-girl voice was still soft, but her laughter was a sharp, cold sound, like ice cubes falling down stairs. "Remind me to invite you should I ever want to play poker," she said. "You're the worst liar I've ever heard."

Harley glanced around for a better weapon and took another step back. "What do you want?"

Abel pushed herself away from the door and walked toward Harley with a smooth, relaxed gait. "I didn't come here on my own," she said. "Cain sent me. He wanted me to have a little chat with you."

"Cain didn't send you," Harley replied quickly.

"Didn't he?" The woman stopped and raised a dark eyebrow. "And how do you know that?"

"Because," said Harley, "Agent Cain is dead."

The woman nodded. "Well, at least you admit that much." Her right hand slipped behind her back for a moment. When she revealed it, her slim fingers were wrapped around a huge dark revolver. She waved the barrel of the gun toward Harley. "Your admission of guilt will make the execution so much cleaner."

"Execution!" Harley dropped her book and stumbled backward. Fear grabbed her as she looked into the dark opening at the end of the heavy gun. "Wait! What are you doing?"

The woman smiled. "Executing the confessed murderer of Agent Ian Cain."

"I'm not a murderer!" Harley cried. "I didn't kill Cain."

Lydia Abel frowned. She lowered the gun for a moment and looked at Harley with a thoughtful expression. "I might think you were lying if I didn't already know you were such a very bad liar." She raised the gun again and sighted along the long barrel. "Or perhaps you were only pretending to be a bad liar."

"I'm telling the truth," Harley protested. "I didn't kill Agent Cain."

The woman lowered the gun again. "Perhaps not," she said. "But we know you were there when he died. If you didn't kill him directly, you did it indirectly."

"I didn't—"

"You did," the woman interrupted. Her voice was still soft, but her tone cut through Harley's protest. "Tell me that you weren't involved in Cain's death. Convince me that this was all a mistake, and I'll walk away."

Harley drew in a deep breath. She hadn't killed Cain, but in a way her actions had certainly contributed to his death. "Cain . . . Cain saved my life. He died trying to save me."

Abel nodded. "And you betrayed him. You left him to die."

"No! I never left him. We were working together. I only—"

"Oh, do be quiet," said the woman. She let the barrel of the gun drift slowly left and right. "Perhaps I should question you at greater length. Headquarters could be very interested in what you have to say."

Harley stared at the gun as it swayed hypnotically back and forth. "Who do you work for?" she asked. "Are you Unit 17? Or Umbra?"

"Neither," replied the woman. "I work for the same people that employed Cain. They sent me here to find you before any more of our operatives met the same fate as Ian Cain."

"That's a lie," said Harley.

"Is it?" The woman seemed to find the statement amusing. The corners of her lips turned up in a smile, and her blue eyes widened.

"Yes." Harley nodded, never taking her eyes from the weapon in the woman's hands. "Cain's organization was nearly destroyed. There's no one left to send you."

The woman in blue shook her head. "The organization is not nearly so damaged as Cain believed. Much of the information he received over the last week of his life was false, passed along by a double agent within our ranks. He even thought that I was dead." She put her thumb against the hammer of the big gun and cocked the weapon. The sound that it made was solid, deep, and utterly terrifying. "We suspect you might have had something to do with that."

"I tried to help Cain." Harley took a step back, putting a little more distance between herself and the woman. The stairs leading to the girls' locker room were only a dozen feet away. Harley wasn't sure that running into the locker room was her best move, but it seemed a lot better than staying where she was and getting killed.

"If you're really from Cain's organization," she asked as she took another step back, "then why don't you have a gun like the one he used?"

The woman raised her left hand and ran a finger slowly down the dark barrel of the revolver. Her lips parted in a smile. "Oh, I have all the little toys," she replied. "But I find that this weapon gets a much more immediate reaction." She brought her right hand up abruptly and directed the heavy gun toward Harley's face. "Don't you think so?"

Harley took another step back. "Yes," she said. There were eight more steps to go.

"Did you know that this was Cain's gun once?" asked the woman in blue. She lowered the gun and cradled it gently in both hands. "It belonged to him when he worked at the FBI."

"So he really was an agent." Harley took another step. And another.

"For over thirty years," said Lydia Abel. "Ian Cain served his country well."

Harley took another step. "That's good."

The woman looked up suddenly. Her blue eyes narrowed. "I would advise you to stay put, Ms. Davisidaro."

A touch of anger colored Harley's fear. "Why?" she asked sharply. "So you can shoot me easier? So you can kill me just because Cain tried to help me?"

For a moment Lydia Abel was so still that she seemed frozen. When she spoke again, her voice was still soft, but there was a raw edge that hadn't been there before. "What was Ian Cain to you?"

Harley clenched her teeth. She had tried to use Cain to get information about her missing father, and Cain had tried to use her to gather information on his damaged organization, but in the end there had been a lot more to their relationship than simply trying to use each other. "He was my friend," she said.

Lydia Abel nodded slowly. "Was he, then?" Her icy blue eyes swept Harley from top to bottom. "Ian was not a man who made a lot of friends."

Harley glanced toward the stairs. They were no more than two yards away. One good jump, and she could be on her way. Instead she turned and took a step toward Lydia Abel. "Cain was my friend. We fought together, and he died saving me."

"I see." Abel's right hand slipped behind her back. When she pulled it into view again, the heavy pistol was gone. "It appears that our information was somewhat in error. Perhaps you didn't kill Ian after all."

"I didn't," Harley insisted.

"I believe you," said Lydia Abel. She looked into Harley's eyes for a moment. "But if, as you say, Agent Cain died to save your life, then you surely must consider yourself in his debt."

An uneasy feeling crept over Harley. "Yes," she admitted. "I do."

"Then you owe the organization a favor," said Lydia Abel. "Be prepared to repay it." Before Harley could respond, the woman swept past her, glided down the stairs toward the locker room, and disappeared through the door.

Harley looked after her in astonishment. "What do you mean?" she called. "Repay it *how?*"

When there was no answer, Harley walked down the steps, pushed open the metal door, and peeked inside. The locker rooms at Stone Harbor High School weren't fancy. The gym was old, and the rooms were little more than a narrow space with a line of benches and rusty metal lockers around a single aisle that led into the shower room. Harley could see the whole area from where she stood. But there was no sign of the woman.

Lydia Abel was gone.

TWO

The van skidded as Scott steered around a curve on the wet highway. He fought the wheel as the rear of the vehicle slid around to the side, sheeting out a wall of rainwater.

"You might consider slowing down," Kenyon suggested with an edge of irritation in his voice.

Scott got the van under control, then glanced over at Kenyon. "You're the one who said we were going to be late for your plane."

"Yes," Kenyon replied with a nod. "We're going to be late because you were slow getting dressed and ready this morning. Killing us now won't make up for it." In his dark blue suit and knotted school tie, Kenyon looked very much like what he was—a very wealthy young man from a very wealthy family. And the expression on his face left no doubt that he was also a very irritated young man.

"I'm not going to kill us," said Scott.

"I'm sure my brother will be sorry to hear that," said Kenyon. "It would make everything so much easier for him." He twisted at his tie for a moment, then turned toward the rain-streaked passenger window. "Next time you should wait until after business is taken care of before you spend the night playing around with your computer schemes."

"But I wasn't playing," Scott protested. He turned his attention back to the road ahead and steered quickly around a slower car. "The new coding was a good idea. It could have led me to Chloe."

"She's been missing for five years," said Kenyon. "Another day won't make any difference."

"It makes a difference to me."

Kenyon snorted. "Great." He folded his arms and leaned back into the van's padded seat. "Well, you better hope you get me to the airport in time, then. Because if I miss this flight, all those fancy computer systems that I paid for will probably be heading back to the store. You'll have a hard time doing any more searches then."

Scott tried to keep his mouth shut. He wanted to keep arguing, but he knew there wasn't any point. The thing that was making Kenyon really angry didn't have anything to do with Scott or with being late for his flight. There was still plenty of time to catch the plane. What was *really* bothering Kenyon was what was waiting at his destination.

Halfway across the country Kenyon's brother was standing by along with a roomful of lawyers. Ever since their parents had been killed in an accident arranged by the secret paramilitary organization Unit 17, Kenyon had been in charge of his parents' company. But Kenyon hadn't exactly tried to keep the company making money. Instead he had spent millions trying to find the people behind Unit 17 and bring them down. Finally his brother and the company's board of directors had moved to put a clamp on Kenyon's cash supply. Unless Kenyon was able to convince them to open up the flow again, money was going to get very tight.

The wet road turned up onto a line of cliffs overlooking the gray Atlantic. Glancing across the whitecapped waves of the bay, Scott could just make out the beach house where Harley Davisidaro had been staying and the buildings of Stone Harbor farther back. In the far distance he even caught a glimpse of Stone Harbor High School before the road curved north again and the town was lost to sight.

Seeing the old brick school building made Scott think about Dee. They had spoken briefly on the phone the night before, but it had been days since they had really talked. Scott could feel the ache of separation. Whenever he was away from Dee for a long time, he felt as though a dark cloud had settled over him. Ever since they had first met, he had loved Dee's quirky smile and sharp humor. Scott could always count on her to come up with a remark that would make him laugh.

After the long, fruitless night of searching the database for Chloe, he definitely needed some cheering up. Scott made a mental note to call Dee as soon as he returned from the airport.

The rainfall increased as they drove north. The gray sky grew so low that it seemed to merge with the highway ahead, and heavy raindrops smacked against the van. Scott tried several times to start a conversation about the storm, or the new security system Kenyon was installing at the house, or the changes he wanted to make in the computer system, but Kenyon barely said a word in reply. He only sat sullenly in his seat, staring out at the rain. After an hour of trying, Scott finally gave up and just drove on in silence.

Stone Harbor was too small to support an airport of its own, and the drive to the nearest city took them the better part of the morning. Despite the rain and the late start they reached the airport with half an hour to spare. Scott pulled the van into the drop-off lane and left the engine idling while Kenyon pushed open the passenger-side door.

"Good luck over there," Scott said.

Kenyon reached back behind his seat and pulled out a black leather garment bag. The expression on his face was so grim, he looked as if he were going to Chicago to face a firing squad. "It's going to take more than luck," he replied.

Scott pushed open his door and walked around to stand beside Kenyon. He searched for something to say. Scott was several inches taller than Kenyon, and they were within a month of the same age, but Kenyon's dark intensity often made Scott feel like a kid. "If you don't get the money," he said, "it'll be all right." He reached out his hand.

"Will it?" Kenyon gave Scott's hand a quick, firm shake. Then he straightened and slung the garment bag over his shoulder. "In the last year I've spent almost four million dollars trying to stop Unit 17 and the other groups. How are we going to fight if we can't afford the tools?"

"All those secret groups have got so much money that it doesn't matter," Scott insisted. "They probably spend four million on their breakfast cereal. If we're going to beat them, it's going to take something more than money."

Kenyon frowned for a moment, then the tight expression on his face eased a little. "I'll remember you said that when we both end up working at the local Burger Jerk." He flashed a quick smile, then stepped away from the van and closed the door.

Scott stood beside the van for a few seconds and watched as Kenyon marched inside and disappeared behind the glass doors of the terminal. He wished he could do something to help Kenyon. Scott had been poor, and he knew they really would get by, but it would be hard on Kenyon.

Scott climbed back inside, shifted the van into gear, and started back toward Stone Harbor. As he drove, his thoughts returned to Dee.

The school day was only half over. Dee was probably stuck in a classroom, listening to some boring lecture. Knowing Dee, he figured she was probably ignoring the lecture and thinking about the dance. Dee had been after Scott to come to a school dance for over a week. It wasn't something Scott was looking forward to—he hated dances and felt very uncomfortable with the idea of hanging around with all the students from Dee's class. But he wanted to see Dee, and if going to the dance was the price, Scott supposed he would just have to pay it.

He wondered for a moment if he could follow Harley's example and go back to school. Scott had made good grades in school—when he went. For the past year he had been too obsessed with searching for Chloe and helping Kenyon to bother with going to school. He certainly didn't miss a lot of the classes, and he had been too shy to ever be popular with the other students. But lately he was sorry he had dropped out. If he ever did have to find a job, he might have a hard time getting computer work without even a high-school diploma to his name. Kenyon's joke about working at Burger Jerk might turn out to be all too true.

The driving rain continued as Scott made his way south along the highway. The ditches alongside the road were full to overflowing, and the northbound cars threw off wakes of water that rolled down the van's windshield in dirty brown sheets. It was an all-around miserable day.

Scott was halfway back to Stone Harbor when he spotted a car pulled over to the curb with its hood raised. It was an old compact car, with patches of rust showing through the fender wells, paint that had faded to the color of peanut shells, and a bumper sticker encouraging people to "Save Chesapeake Bay." Even with all the rain pouring down, Scott could see clouds of steam boiling out from the corners of the car's hood. It was obvious the vehicle was going nowhere fast. A man in a rain-soaked T-shirt stood in front of the car, staring down at the vehicle with a heartsick expression.

Scott slowed, drove past the stalled car, then

pulled over to the side of the road. He lowered the van's window and leaned his head out into the pouring rain. "Having trouble?" he called.

The man left the front of the car and jogged toward Scott. He was a middle-aged man with a pale, doughy face and thin hair that had been pressed to his skull by the rain. He wore glasses with heavy black frames. His face was turned down in what seemed to be a permanent frown. "Having nothing *but* trouble," he replied as he came up beside the van. "As usual."

"Do you need me to call a mechanic?" Scott offered.

The man gave a bitter laugh. "I need you to call a junkyard." He jerked a thumb toward the steaming car. "It's time to put that thing in a crusher."

"How about a lift?" asked Scott.

The man's sad face lightened a little. "You going anywhere near Stone Harbor?"

Scott smiled. "I'm not only going near it," he said, "I'm going straight to it. Hop in if you want to come along."

The man sprouted a smile, but his sunken, red eyes still looked sad. "All right, let me get something from my car and I'll be right there." He turned and jogged back through the driving rain.

Scott watched in the rearview mirror as the man reached inside the stalled car and pulled out a small suitcase. If Kenyon had been there, the man wouldn't be getting his ride. In fact, Scott doubted that Kenyon would have even stopped. It wasn't that Kenyon was cruel, though he did sometimes forget that there were other people in the world besides himself. Kenyon wouldn't have stopped because he was always thinking about security. The boy was seriously paranoid. He would have looked at the idea of letting a total stranger into the car as completely insane.

The man hurried to the van with the suitcase dangling from his right hand. Scott flipped the lock switch and let him in.

"You don't know how much I appreciate this," the man said. He climbed into the passenger seat and sat, dripping water onto the floorboard.

"No problem," Scott replied. "Your car going to be all right here?"

The man grunted. "If someone wants to steal it, they better bring a tow truck."

Scott pulled out onto the highway and started down the rain-slick road. The stranded car vanished behind sheets of rain and mist. "I guess you can send someone for it once you get to Stone Harbor."

"Once I get to Stone Harbor, I might not be going anywhere for a while," said the man.

"Are you visiting relatives?" Scott asked.

The stranger was slow to answer. "You might say that," he replied after several seconds. "Relatives that I haven't seen in a long time."

Scott nodded. "I'm sure they'll be glad to see you."

The man shrugged. He took off his damp glasses and rubbed them against his equally damp shirt. "I'm not so sure about that," he said. "We lost touch a long time ago. They might have forgotten all about me."

"I doubt it," Scott replied. He thought of Chloe. It had been almost six years since she had disappeared, but she had never been out of his thoughts for more than a day.

"Let's hope you're right." The man leaned back in his seat and ran his fingers through the thin strands of his wet hair. "I'm not sure they'll even remember me."

Scott frowned. In all the time he had been looking for Chloe, he had rarely stopped to wonder if she was looking for him. Maybe he would find her someday, and she wouldn't even remember him. "No," he said aloud. "They'll remember you."

"Let's hope so." The man dropped his suitcase onto the floor and leaned toward Scott with his right hand extended. "I want to thank you again for stopping. It means a lot to me."

Scott took one hand off the wheel and shook the stranger's hand. "I couldn't let you sit there and drown."

"A lot of people could," said the man. "Let me introduce myself. I'm Gunter Rhinehardt."

"Nice to meet you," said Scott. "I'm . . ." His voice faded and his eyes widened as he realized what the man had said.

Scott slammed the brakes. The van skidded sideways on the wet road, came within inches of sliding into the ditch, then splashed to a halt. Scott twisted around in his seat and stared at the man in the passenger chair. "You're *Gunter Rhinehardt?*"

The man nodded calmly. "That's right."

For a moment Scott was too confused to speak.

Finally he found his voice. "You were there. You were at the Benevolence Home."

"Yes," the stranger said with another nod. "I was there."

"You were one of the guards. You were on duty the night—"

"The night that Chloe Adair disappeared," the man finished. "Yes, that was me."

Scott shook his head slowly. He studied the features of the man in the passenger seat. This man seemed so much older than the guard Scott remembered from the orphanage. "You're not Rhinehardt," he said at last. "Rhinehardt was taller."

"No," the man replied. "You were shorter, Scott."

"You know me?"

"Of course." The man took off his glasses and wiped them again on his wet shirt. "You're the one I was coming to see in Stone Harbor."

"Me?" Scott leaned away from the man. He thought for a moment that Kenyon was right—you should never stop for strangers. "You're not my family," he said. "You were just a guard."

Rhinehardt shrugged. "There's more to it than you know. Our relationship is deeper than it seemed."

A cold chill crept over Scott, and he suddenly shivered. He glanced out the rain-streaked window, then looked over at the suitcase in front of the former guard. They were still miles away from Stone Harbor, and the case was large enough to hold any sort of weapon. If the man decided to attack, there was no one around to stop

42

him but Scott. "You're one of them," he said softly.

"Them?"

Scott nodded. "You know. You're from one of the secret groups."

Rhinehardt's frown deepened, but after a moment he nodded. "Yes," he replied. "I am from a secret organization."

"And you're here to kill me," said Scott.

The man shook his head furiously. "No! I'm not here to harm you in any way. In fact, I'm here to help."

Scott blinked in confusion. "Help? Help with what?"

Rhinehardt leaned forward in his seat and turned his face up toward the rainy sky. "Your inquiries into the present whereabouts of Chloe Adair have not gone unnoticed. It seems that you have acquired information from some hidden source."

"I don't know what you're talking about," Scott said quickly. The information he had been using to search for Chloe had come from a database found in the lair of a dead Umbra agent, but he wasn't about to confess this to Rhinehardt.

The former guard turned to face Scott. "I have information of my own."

A touch of excitement penetrated Scott's fear. "Information about Chloe?"

The man nodded. "Yes. If we pool what we know, then I believe there's a very good chance we could find her."

Rhinehardt's words seemed to hang in the air. Scott

43

looked at the former guard and shook his head slowly. The idea of finding Chloe was painfully attractive, but the risk was too great. "How do I know if I can trust you?"

"Do you know how hard I've been looking for her?" Rhinehardt asked. There was raw, trembling emotion in the man's voice. "Do you know how I've spent almost every day of the last five years trying to find out where Chloe had gone?"

"Why?" asked Scott. "So you can use her in some sick experiment?"

"Of course not!" cried Rhinehardt. Even through the heavy glasses Scott could see the intense look in the man's eyes. "Chloe's very important. More important than you could possibly understand. Her safe return is all that matters."

Scott looked into the man's eyes for a moment longer. Around them the storm grew stronger. Wind buffeted the side of the van, and rain smashed against the windshield as if someone had opened up a fire hose. "Chloe is important to me," Scott said at last. "But that's because she was my friend. Why is she so important to you?"

Gunter Rhinehardt folded his hands together and bowed his head. "Because Chloe Adair is the end result of over five hundred years and twenty-three generations of work," he said solemnly. "She is the ultimate product of Legion."

THREE

Dee opened the glove compartment of her ancient car and watched as a stream of water and damp paper spilled out onto the floor.

"Wonderful." She groaned as she fished her registration papers out of the soggy mess. She held the pink sheet of paper carefully between her fingers and scowled as the water streamed away. "Another day in paradise."

Harley peered into the car from the passenger side and frowned at the puddle of water on the seat. "Does this happen often?"

"Only when it rains," said Dee. "I think one of the rust holes in the hood is letting water in under the dashboard. I'd have it fixed, but I'm saving up to replace the water pump before it breaks down completely."

"Have you ever thought about getting rid of this thing?" asked Harley. "I know it was cheap, but it's always breaking down. You're going to spend a fortune just keeping it running."

"Shhh!" Dee hissed. She patted the hood of the battered AMC Gremlin, then walked around the car to stand next to Harley. "Are you kidding? This is a great car, a wonderful car!" She leaned closer and spoke in a whisper. "Careful, don't let it hear you saying bad things. That only makes it grumpy."

"I wouldn't want to do that." Harley looked up at

45

the sky. "Now that the rain has stopped, maybe I should just walk home."

Dee shook her head. "You don't have to walk. The seat will dry out in a minute and I'll give you a ride."

Harley glanced through the window again. "I think it'll take more like a week." She straightened and pushed a stray lock of dark hair away from her face. "Besides, I need the exercise."

Dee laughed. "You need exercise? You're already the healthiest person on the planet. If you exercise any more, you'll probably go into negative numbers and start getting flabby."

A ghost of a smile crossed Harley's lips, but it died quickly. She turned and looked toward the school. "I think I should do more running."

"Oh, come on," said Dee. "You already look too good. Next to you I'm a walking ad for fat."

"You are not fat." Again Harley started to smile, but it rapidly faded. She glanced at the school again. "I just need to run," she said.

"Is something wrong?" asked Dee.

Harley shrugged. "Just more nerves, I guess."

Dee looked hard into her friend's dark eyes. "What happened to you this afternoon? You haven't been the same since we talked after second period."

"It's nothing. Really." Harley smiled again, but this time the expression looked as artificial as plastic fruit. "I haven't been putting in enough miles lately. Running home will be good for me."

"In your jeans?"

Harley nodded. "It'll be okay. See you in the morning!" She waved quickly, turned, and jogged away across the parking lot.

Dee stood and watched as Harley hurried around the corner of the school and out of sight. Something was wrong. Dee couldn't be sure exactly what had happened, but something had spooked Harley between the time they had talked that morning and the end of the school day. She looked up at the dark windows of the school. Harley might have been bothered by one of the guys acting like a jerk, but Dee didn't think so. After everything that Harley had been through, she wasn't likely to be psyched out by idiots like Jason Edwards.

Whatever was wrong, Dee knew she wasn't going to solve it by standing around the parking lot. She peeled her damp registration papers from the top of the car, frowned at the smear of ink that had once been her name, and climbed into the aging vehicle. The Gremlin might be old and ugly as sin, but it had a huge engine. Dee smiled as the eight cylinder roared to life. With a tap of the gas she skidded out of the parking lot and headed through the center of Stone Harbor.

She thought for a moment about driving straight out to the mansion that Kenyon had been renting so she could pay a visit to Scott, but a rumble in her stomach encouraged her to head for home first. When possible, she always tried to eat before going to see Scott. That way she never had to pig out in front of him.

It took Dee less than five minutes to reach her home. She hurried out of the car and pushed open the kitchen door with her mind on a cheesecake that was lurking in the fridge. But what she found instead was her father.

She stopped in the doorway. "What are you doing here?"

Chief of Police Charles Janes leaned back in his chair. "That's not the friendliest greeting I ever got," he said. He was still wearing his khaki police uniform with the silver star on the chest. His soft tan hat lay on the table next to a bowl of apples.

Dee smiled at her father. "Sorry, Dad. I just didn't expect to see you home at this time of the day."

"Can't a man come home early to see his favorite daughter?" Dee's father reached out and picked up a glossy red apple from the bowl.

Dee narrowed her eyes. "You were never good at this game, Dad. What's wrong?"

Her father tossed the apple into the air, caught it, and set it down on the table. "I'm glad the people I arrest can't see through me as easily as you do." He tipped up the corner of his hat and revealed sheets of folded paper. "I'm afraid there's more trouble for your friend Harley."

"Harley?" Dee pulled out a chair at the end of the table and sat down across from her father. "Did something happen at school today?"

Her father shook his head. "Not that I know of. Why?"

"Nothing, really," said Dee. "Harley just seemed scared of something."

"She *should* be scared." Dee's father pulled one of the sheets of paper from the table and passed it across to Dee. "This came through the fax about noon today."

Dee dropped her car keys on the end of the table. She unfolded the sheet of paper and found herself looking at a picture of Harley Davisidaro.

The word at the top of the sheet read "Wanted." The picture of Harley wasn't very flattering. In fact, it did a pretty good job of making her look angry and threatening. Kathleen Elise Davisidaro, read the letters below the picture. This Suspect Is Wanted in Connection with Murder, Theft, and Destruction of Public Property. Dee dropped the sheet on the table.

"Unit 17 has been putting out wanted posters for Harley ever since her father disappeared," she said. "There's nothing new about this."

"Harley's been wanted," Dee's father agreed, "but all the previous posters were very careful to say she was only wanted for questioning. This time she's listed as a suspect in a murder."

Dee bit her lip and looked down at the glossy fax. "That makes a difference?"

Her father nodded. "It'll make a big difference. When it comes to murder, every little deputy in every little town will be paying attention. If Harley should be stopped for a traffic ticket or jaywalking, the odds are pretty high that someone is going to remember seeing her picture."

"That doesn't sound good," Dee admitted, "but as long as Harley stays here, she should be safe. You put together that story about the witness protection program, and you made sure all the local posters were taken down. She's safe in Stone Harbor, right?"

The expression on her father's face was enough to tell Dee that more bad news was coming. "Not exactly," he said. He put a finger on top of the next sheet of paper and slid it along the table toward Dee. "This came in around two."

Dee took the paper and turned it over. At first she thought it was identical to the first sheet. There were the same big letters at the top, the same list of charges at the bottom, and the same picture of a sullen, criminal Harley in between. She was about to ask her father what was wrong with the page when she spotted it for herself. "This one doesn't say Kathleen Davisidaro."

Dee's father nodded. He took the paper from her hands and read aloud. "Kathleen Elise Vincent."

"But how can they know that?" Dee asked. "Agent Cain gave that name to Harley. He provided her with a new driver's license, birth certificate—everything."

"I don't know who knows or how they know," her father replied, "but someone has figured out this little trick of Cain's. If Kathleen Vincent's name ends up in any kind of database, Harley is going to be hauled away."

Dee stood up quickly. "I've got to warn her." She snatched up her keys and turned toward the back door.

"Hold on!" called her father. "Don't rush off."

Dee looked at him over her shoulder. "But I have to warn her."

Her father frowned. "Ten minutes won't make a difference. Sit down."

There was a hardness in his voice. Dee had often heard her father use that iron tone with prisoners or with the deputies under his command, but he had very rarely used it with her. She went back to the table and sat.

"What is it?" she asked. "Is something else wrong?"

"Yes," her father replied with a nod. "It's you."

Dee frowned in surprise. "Me?"

Her father looked at her with a intensity that made Dee squirm in her chair. "I know you've been lying to me," he said.

"I never—"

"Be quiet." His voice was soft, but the iron tone was still there. "Ever since Harley came to town, you've been trying to help her."

"But she needs someone to help her," Dee said quickly. "Her father was kidnapped, and all these people have been after her, and someone has to watch out for her."

Her father sighed. "I agree. That's why I put her up here at our own house after Noah Templer disappeared. That's why I've lied to half the people in town about who she is and what she's doing in Stone Harbor." He shook his head slowly. "That has to end."

One of the biggest constants in her life was the pride Dee felt in her father. He had been a policeman since before she was born, and for as long as Dee could remember she had wanted to be like her father. She had even thought about going into police work when she graduated. But as she listened to his words, she felt a wash of burning disappointment. "You're going to abandon her," she said. "You're going to throw Harley to a bunch of murdering lunatics."

"I'm not out to kill her," Dee's father replied firmly. "You don't know how much I wish we could just open up the spare bedroom and let her move in. Your mother and I both care deeply about the girl."

"Then why are you going to let them catch her?" asked Dee.

Her father picked up his felt hat from the table and ran his finger along the soft brim. "I hope no one catches her," he said, "but I'm done lying to my men." His gray eyes turned back to Dee. "And I'm done risking you."

"You're not risking me."

"That's where you're wrong," he replied. "Twice now you've disappeared. Once for three days, once for four. Where did you go?"

Dee closed her mouth. She had told her parents something of the trips she had made to Washington, D.C., and St. Louis in her efforts to help Harley and Noah, but she hadn't told them much. Besides, most of what she had told them hadn't exactly been the truth. Sometimes Dee wasn't even sure *she* knew the truth. The things that had happened on those trips were too weird to believe.

"I was just trying to help," she said after a moment.

Her father nodded. "I know you were, and helping

your friends is an admirable trait." He flipped his hat over and dropped it on top of his head. "But no matter how admirable I think it is, it will be no comfort to your mother when we're attending your funeral."

"That's just plain stupid," Dee protested. "I'm not going to get killed."

"Don't make promises you can't keep." Her father stood up. "I know the kind of people that are in this Unit 17, and I can imagine what the other groups you've talked about are like. None of them would hesitate for one moment before they cut you in half."

"But—" started Dee.

Her father held up his hand and cut her off. "I don't want to hear it," he said. "Starting today, you're going to cut back on your contact with Harley Davisidaro."

Dee felt her throat tighten. She hadn't cried in front of her father since she was ten years old, but she could feel the tears drawing close. "I have to help her."

"No," said her father. "Go to her today. Warn her. Then stay away. And the same thing goes for your two new friends, Kenyon and Scott."

Dee's eyes widened in shock. "I can't stay away from Scott. Nobody's putting out wanted posters about him."

"Not yet," her father replied. "But both of them are involved with the same people that are after Harley. It's only a matter of time before they come here."

Dee faced her father in silence for a few long seconds, then she slowly shook her head. "No," she said. "I won't do it."

Her father stepped closer and leaned down until the brim of his hat was almost touching her forehead. "You *will* do it," he said in his iron voice. "I don't care if I have to take away your car. I don't care if I have to escort you home from school. I don't care if I have to lock you in your room and feed you through the keyhole until you're thirty. You're going to get away from this insanity, and you're going to be all right, and you're going to college in the fall. Understand?"

I understand, Dee thought. But she made no answer.

Her father straightened and adjusted his hat. "For now you'll still see Harley at school. Go say your goodbyes to the others." He turned and headed out the door.

For minutes after he left, Dee stood in the middle of the kitchen and stared at the open door. It was true enough that she had lied to her father. If she had told him about all the things that had happened over the past few months and all the times someone really *had* tried to kill her, Dee figured that her father might carry through on his threat to lock her in her room.

Dee imagined that all teenagers probably lied to their parents about something. Of course, most of them were probably lying about staying out too late or what they did on their dates. She doubted there were many kids out there who were hiding encounters with secret societies and inhuman killers.

Even though she had lied to her parents, Dee couldn't remember a time when she had directly disobeyed them. Her mother and father were strong people and fair people.

Listening to them had always seemed like a good idea.

But this time Dee knew her father was wrong. There was no reason to stay away from Scott and Kenyon, and leaving Harley to face the secret groups on her own was just plain unfair. Dee tightened her hand around her car keys. This time it was going to take more than lying.

"Time to grow up," she said to the empty room. Then she headed out to warn Harley.

55

FOUR

Harley jogged over the damp sandy soil along the shoulder of the highway.

Dee had been right—the jeans she was wearing kept her from really stretching out and running at high speed. She wasn't even wearing a decent pair of running shoes. But even though she was just taking it easy, Harley felt something of the warm, comfortable feeling she sometimes got while running.

When she was younger, Harley had been dragged from school to school as her father moved from one military base to another to pursue his research. There had never been enough time to make close friends or to get really involved in anything that required other people, but she could always run. It had become her private sanctuary—her only way of escaping when things were going bad. After all the horrifying things that had happened over the last few months, Harley was relieved to find that running could still bring her closer to peace.

The beach house where she had been staying was almost three miles out of town. Between the bad shoes and the tight jeans, it probably would have made better sense to wait for Dee's car to dry out or to just sit down in the puddle and get wet. But a strange feeling had come over her back at the school—the terrible feeling that someone was watching her.

No matter what Dee said, Harley knew there was more to this strange sensation than just being scoped out by a bunch of sophomores. If she had learned anything over the past months, it was to trust her feelings. More than once her intuition had been the only thing that kept her alive. The feeling that had come over her while standing beside Dee's car had been the strongest yet, so strong that it was almost a physical sensation—a soft electric tingling along her spine.

Now that she was away from the old brick school, she felt a little better. Getting away from school was part of it, but the old magic of running helped a lot. With every step her tight muscles loosened and the warm ache of exercise grew stronger.

For the hundredth time in a month Harley promised herself that she was going to get back into a regular schedule of training.

Starting today, she thought. No more putting it off. As soon as she got home she was going to change into shorts and decent running shoes and do a couple of miles along the beach.

Harley pushed herself to run a little faster as the road curved around and headed down a long slope toward the beach. The houses began to thin out as the last of the new subdivisions gave way to the older homes that had been built by generations of fishermen. Off to her right she could see the burned remains of the Fun World amusement park. Most of Fun World had been destroyed when a pair of assassins tried to trap Harley there and kill her.

Crews had moved in to clean up the charred refreshment stands and the twisted remains of the collapsed roller coaster, but so far there was no new construction. It looked to Harley as if Fun World wasn't going to be very fun that summer.

Halfway down the long slope the tingling sensation of being watched returned. Harley twisted her head around and looked back over her shoulder. At first she saw nothing. Then she spotted a black sedan creeping slowly between the houses at the top of the hill.

The tingling sensation turned into a cold feeling in the pit of Harley's stomach. Unit 17 had driven cars like the one behind her. Twice Harley had found herself trapped inside Unit 17 bases, and twice those bases had ended up in ruins. If Unit 17 were after her, she didn't expect they were coming over for dinner.

Harley turned away from the car, lowered her head, and ran on at double speed. She sprinted for a block, then glanced back again. The car was still behind her. It was still moving slowly along the side of the road, but not as slowly as it had been when she first spotted it. Even though Harley was running faster, the car was drawing closer.

Running had been enough to get Harley's heart beating fast. Seeing the car gaining on her made her heart start to race. She abruptly turned off the road and ran through the narrow alley between two houses. She dodged around a backyard swimming pool, forced herself through a ragged hedge, and emerged on a side street. She paused for a second and looked back toward the highway. She saw no sign of the black sedan.

Harley drew in a deep breath. It was possible that it had all been a mistake. The sedan might have just been looking for an address. It might not have had anything to do with Harley. But she didn't want to bet her life on it.

When the sedan failed to appear after another few seconds, Harley jogged to the end of the street and slipped into the tangled woods that covered the hillside. From there she worked her way back into the deep shadows of the woods until the houses behind her were out of sight, then she began to move downhill toward the beach.

As she picked her way through patches of tight undergrowth and pulled briers from her clothes, Harley felt a powerful flash of déjà vu. It seemed to her that she had been in this place before. In fact, it seemed that she was *always* trapped in the wilderness, always being pursued by some secret group that wanted to kill her. Always on the run.

She stopped in the middle of the dark woods and clenched her hands in anger. She was just so tired of it all. Dee had tried to convince Harley that she could go back to school and be an ordinary student. Obviously that wasn't true. Already she had come close to being killed by Lydia Abel, and now someone else was after her. Her life was a long way from normal, and it didn't seem to be getting any better. At least when this whole thing had started, Noah had been there to share the terror and the danger. Dee, Kenyon, and Scott might know what was going on, but she didn't feel as close to any of them as she had felt—still felt—to Noah Templer.

Harley looked around the silent forest, sighed, and moved on.

By the time she picked her way through the dense woods, the sun had dropped down to touch the line of hills to the west. Harley emerged onto the edge of the coastal highway a half mile from the beach house and stepped clear of the woods. She peered back and forth along the roadway. There was some traffic running north out of Stone Harbor and a few cars heading south, but she saw no sign of any black sedans.

Harley walked slowly toward the beach house. Running had made her feel better, but struggling through the thick woods had been exhausting. The idea of going out and running a few miles along the beach no longer sounded like nearly as much fun as it had a few hours before.

A hot shower, she thought as she walked up the sandy drive to the small house. Or better yet, a long soak in the tub. Some candles were stowed away in the beach house. She would turn off all the lights and lie in the hot sudsy water with only a candle to brighten the room. Harley felt better just thinking about it. She fumbled out her keys, opened the door, and stepped inside.

"Ah, Ms. Davisidaro," said a man's voice from across the living room. "I was beginning to worry about you."

Harley froze in the doorway. For a moment an electric current of fear surged through her limbs and she almost turned and ran. But the moment passed. The wave of anger she had felt in the woods came rushing back and drove away the fear like water burning off a hot skillet. There was someone waiting for her wherever she went, and it was time to stop running.

She squinted into the shadows of the dark living room. "Who are you?"

A light snapped on across the room. In the bright yellow glow Harley saw a stocky middle-aged man standing beside the couch. He had a heavily creased face and dark hair that was shot through with silver. His clothing was plain, almost drab—a dark gray suit, a crisp white shirt, and a black tie crossed with bands of silver—but the way the clothes were cut was enough to show that they hadn't come off the rack at a discount store.

"Agent Kent Morris," said the man. "I'm from the NSA."

Harley studied the stranger's craggy face. "NSA?"

The man slipped his hand into the jacket of his suit and produced a black leather billfold. With a flick of his wrist he opened the billfold to reveal a plastic photo identification card and a badge featuring a glittering silver eagle. "National Security Agency," he explained.

Harley squinted at the badge. It was too far away to read, but she was in no mood to get closer. "That still doesn't mean anything to me," she said. "What's the National Security Agency?"

"That's a surprisingly common reaction," said Agent Morris. He flipped the badge closed again and returned it to his jacket. "We're an agency of the federal government, charged with protecting certain areas of vital national interest from our enemies. We often deal with cryptography and computer crime, but every now and then we have to get our hands dirty."

Harley glanced left and right. The man seemed to be alone. If it came time to fight or run away, she thought she would have a pretty good chance. She stepped the rest of the way into the room and eased the front door closed. "I thought the CIA protected the government," she said.

Morris shook his head. "The CIA gathers information and may help out when it comes to the occasional terrorist. The FBI tackles criminals." He reached into his jacket again, but this time instead of a billfold he came out with a cellophane-wrapped pack of cigarettes. "Threats to this nation come in a great number of forms," he continued as he peeled the wrapper from the pack. "As I'm sure you're aware, not all of them fit into neat categories."

"Don't," said Harley.

Agent Morris froze. "Don't what?"

Harley nodded toward the cigarettes. "This is my place. I don't allow anyone to smoke in here."

The NSA agent hesitated for a moment, then dropped the pack onto the coffee table. "All right," he said. He waved toward the couch. "But do you mind if I sit down?"

"Be my guest," Harley replied. She felt pleased with herself for standing up to the man.

"Thank you." Agent Morris stepped around in front of the couch and settled against the cushions. For a big man who was obviously past his prime, Morris moved with unusual ease and smoothness. "As I was saying, the NSA is required to address some rather *obscure* issues."

Harley nodded. "So you're a secret agency, like Unit 17."

The NSA man's face gathered in a frown and an edge of irritation entered his voice. "Hardly. For one thing, the NSA is not a secret agency. We are an open, publicly funded agency that reports directly to the president of the United States. If you had paid attention to the news, you would surely know who we are."

Harley tightened her jaw. She was in no mood to be lectured. "You'll have to excuse me," she said. "I haven't had a lot of time for doing my social studies lately."

Agent Morris looked at her for a moment, and Harley thought she detected a trace of a smile. "Maybe not," he said, "but you should understand that Unit 17 differs from us in another very important way—Unit 17 is out of control."

The agent's words were interesting, but it was his tone that really interested Harley. Just the way he said "Unit 17" carried a truckload of emotion—emotion that said clearly enough that Agent Morris put Unit 17 into a category with slugs, mold, and spoiled meat. It was an attitude that gave Harley some hope, but she didn't want to jump to any conclusions. "What do you mean?" she asked carefully. "How is Unit 17 out of control?"

"I think you have a very good idea what I mean, Ms. Davisidaro," replied the agent. He leaned back against the couch cushions and looked off into the corner of the room. "Unit 17 was started after World War II. The government came into possession of certain, well, let's just say *extraordinary* artifacts, and they needed somebody to investigate. Unit 17 got the job. Then in the sixties Unit 17 was involved with CIA experiments in telepathy. For years they were regarded as something of a joke, but a few years ago they began to show results. Big results."

Harley walked slowly across the room and sat down on a chair across the table from Agent Morris. "Because of my father."

"Yes," he replied with a nod. "It seems that your father's work was instrumental in pushing Unit 17 into new avenues of research. They began to demand, and receive, greater levels of funding, more people, everything they asked for." Morris paused for a moment and glanced across the table at Harley. From close up she could see that the agent's eyes were a strange, cloudy gray. "I don't have to tell you that some of the research produced by Unit 17 was very impressive," he continued. "The folks over at the Pentagon were so excited, they were willing to give them anything. Absolutely anything. Half a dozen other black ops projects were scrapped to stoke the fire under Unit 17."

Harley nodded. She had seen what it was like inside a Unit 17 base. The technology there had been so advanced that it was like looking at equipment from another world. Most of what she had seen was aimed at perfecting her father's most complex invention—the white sphere.

The sphere could act as a transport, moving people between any two points on earth in an instant. Or it could serve as a gateway between worlds. It could be the most important invention in history. But in the hands of men like those who controlled Unit 17, it could also be a terrible weapon. Compared to the sphere, the most advanced missiles and aircraft were like wooden spears and stone-tipped arrows. The sphere could deliver a bomb anywhere, and no security system could stop it. With a sphere someone could place a grenade inside the Oval Office—or a knife into the heart of an enemy.

Harley wasn't sure how to feel about her father's involvement in the project. She was certain that her father couldn't have known how Unit 17 intended to use his work. She couldn't believe that he could have worked so long and so hard only to put the ultimate weapon in the hands of people who were ready to use it. On the other hand, her father's journals had revealed that he knew a lot of things that he had never told Harley—including the truth about what had happened to her mother. As long as her father and Noah were both lost inside the mysterious, endless worlds within the sphere, Harley would never know the whole story.

Agent Morris reached toward the table and picked up the pack of cigarettes. Then he seemed to realize what he was doing and dropped them again. "I've been trying to stop," he muttered, shaking his head. "But a forty-year-old habit is hard to break."

"What about Unit 17?" asked Harley. "How did they get out of control?"

"It took us a couple of years to even find out that they were," said Morris. He rubbed his right hand along his chin. "When a program operates with the kind of secrecy that surrounds Unit 17, there's not a lot of supervision. By the time the government realized they were no longer working for us, they had built up their own structure of secret connections. We don't even know where else they may have a base or how much of our money they might have stored away in some numbered bank account."

If the idea wasn't so frightening, Harley would have laughed. "That seems like a wonderful way to run a government."

Agent Morris shrugged. "You're welcome to try your hand at doing better," he said, "but first we need to bring Unit 17 down, or there may not be any United States government left."

Harley frowned. "What do you mean?"

"Think about it," said Morris. "Who threatens the existence of Unit 17? Not the Russians. Not the Chinese. It's us. They know we're trying to shut them down." His cloudy eyes took on the glint of cold metal. "Their only chance at survival is to take us out first."

A fresh brand of fear tightened Harley's guts. "How is that possible?" she asked. "No matter how much money you've given Unit 17, they can't be a match for the whole army, navy, and air force."

"Don't forget the marines," said Agent Morris. A hard smile crossed his lips, but it vanished almost as soon as it came. "I wish you were right, but I think you know that Unit 17 has a weapon that can make them more than a match for anything we can throw their way."

Harley swallowed. "The sphere."

Agent Morris nodded. "Yes. We didn't even know that Unit 17 was close to having an operational sphere until a few months ago. Now that we understand what such a device is capable of, we have to take any steps possible to stop them."

"But . . . the equipment Unit 17 needs to make the sphere is gone," said Harley. "There's no danger now."

The NSA agent stared at Harley in silence for a few moments. "We know of the destruction of the base here and of other events on the base near Washington. I take it you're already familiar with these events?"

Harley wasn't sure what to say. Agent Morris seemed to know a lot about her father and about Unit 17's plans, but it wasn't clear how much he knew about Harley or any of the things that had happened to her since her father's disappearance. "I know a little something about what's been happening," she admitted at last.

Morris nodded. "We suspected that you had been involved with events over the past few weeks. But I'm afraid your information isn't quite complete—Unit 17 has almost finished a new facility. In a matter of days they'll be able to generate a sphere."

The news brought Harley a mixture of hope and fear. If Unit 17 was able to generate a white sphere, they would have a terrible power in their control. But the sphere also provided the gateway to the place where Noah and her father lay waiting. If Unit 17 really did generate a new portal, there was a chance that they might be able to escape. Somehow she didn't think that the NSA was going to be very concerned about Noah and her father.

"What are you going to do about it?" she asked. "Blow up the base?"

Agent Morris shook his head. "It's not that simple," he said. "The government has enough information to know that Unit 17 is very close to being ready to go. What the government is not aware of is the location of the Unit 17 facility."

Even if Noah and her father did escape from the sphere, Harley didn't expect them to get a very friendly greeting at some secret Unit 17 base. A new idea occurred to her.

"Maybe everything is going to be okay," said Harley. "Even if Unit 17 has all the gear, they can't make the sphere operate without using someone with very special powers."

To her disappointment, Agent Morris only nodded. "Yes, we're aware of that requirement, but our understanding is that Unit 17 is very close to acquiring the person they need."

Harley frowned. "So what are you going to do?" she asked. "If you can't find the base, how can you stop them?"

The NSA agent leaned forward on the couch. "We have a way," he said. "And we're going to need your help."

"*My* help?" Harley leaned back in surprise. "Why?"

Agent Morris stood up and took a step toward Harley. "We're going to build a sphere of our own. And we need you to power it for us."

Scott watched as Gunter Rhinehardt examined the computer room.

"This is your facility?" the man from Legion asked. "I'm really amazed that you've managed to do so much with so little."

"So little?" Scott shook his head, puzzled. "There's enough gear in here to run NASA."

"Oh, of course." Rhinehardt walked along the bank of computers. He reached down, touched one of the keyboards, and gave an amused smile. "But it's all off-the-shelf equipment, isn't it? There's nothing here that couldn't be purchased in any computer store."

The man's statement irritated Scott. "This is the cutting edge."

Rhinehardt glanced at him over his shoulder. "The cutting edge for *most* people," he corrected Scott. "Don't get me wrong—I'm not trying to insult you. I'm actually very impressed that you managed to accomplish so much with such . . . primitive machines."

Scott frowned. Bringing the Legion agent into the house was a terrible risk. He had little doubt that once Rhinehardt had gained all the knowledge from Scott's computer, he would try to leave. If Scott hoped to see Chloe, he would have to watch the Legion agent every second and be ready in case the man tried to escape.

If Kenyon were there to see what was going on, he

would have had a fit. It wasn't just data on Chloe that was contained in the computer's files—everything that Scott and Kenyon had learned about the secret organizations was stored in the system. If Kenyon knew that Scott was letting an agent of one of those groups near the computer system, he would probably kick *both* of them out. Or shoot them. Or kick them out and then shoot them.

"Uh," Scott said nervously. "If your computer is so much better than mine, why don't we use it?"

Rhinehardt nodded. "We'll use both," he said. "I need the data you have stored in your system, and you need the search algorithms built into mine. Together we'll find our missing Chloe." He dropped into the swivel chair in front of the computer system.

Hearing the former guard talk about Chloe that way gave Scott a strange feeling. "I still can't believe Chloe is some kind of clone," he said softly.

"Not a clone," replied Rhinehardt. "She was carefully constructed from the best genetic material taken from generation twenty-two. She was assembled gene by gene."

The whole idea made Scott feel a little queasy. Chloe had been his closest friend. Finding out that she was part of some monster science experiment was like finding out that he had grown up in a test tube. "There was a guy here in Stone Harbor that—"

"Noah Templer," Rhinehardt interjected. The Legion agent reached down and threw the main power switch. All around the room computer monitors began to glow. "Yes, Noah was another of ours. He was a secondary offshoot of generation twenty-two, using a few advanced alleles."

"What?"

Rhinehardt spun around in the chair. "Think of it in terms of computer software," he said. "Chloe is version twenty-three. There was a version twenty-two released about ten years before. Noah is something in between, a beta version of generation twenty-three."

"A beta," Scott repeated. Somehow thinking of people as computer software didn't make it sound any better. He had a vision of a huge computer store where row after row of people stood waiting in shrink-wrapped packages.

Rhinehardt took another look at the computer screens, then nodded. "Right," he said. "Now we need to bring out my system and interface the two."

"Can't you just add the search algorithms to my system?" asked Scott.

The Legion agent shook his head. "It's not that simple. You've been searching the actual text, right?"

"Sure," Scott replied with a nod. "What else is there to search?"

"Patterns," said Rhinehardt. He reached out and tapped his index finger against the screen. "Right now this computer is displaying a simple interface. A few icons. A little text. But a wealth of information is here that you can't see."

Scott frowned. He had stared at the same display a thousand times, but he had no idea what Rhinehardt was talking about. "What information?"

"It's hidden in a hundred places." Rhinehardt ran his fingertip along the screen. "Minor variations in pixel brightness. Secondary scan pages. Fluctuations of the screen boundary."

"But all those things are random," Scott protested.

"They *appear* random. But only because you don't have the proper system to decode the information they contain." Rhinehardt grabbed the mouse and moved the pointer across the screen. With a click he started a Web browser. "The Internet is especially rich in this additional information. Haven't you ever wondered why your computer system can't communicate as fast as it's supposed to?"

"That's because of noise on the line," Scott replied.

The Legion agent smiled. "It's not noise. It's us."

Scott stared at the central monitor. "You're saying that every computer in the world is loaded with invisible information?"

Rhinehardt nodded. "Not all the time, of course. But very much of it." He slid the mouse again and scrolled quickly through a screen of text. "For every piece of text or every picture that you see transmitted over the Internet, there is a hundred times as much hidden data being transmitted."

"That's not possible," Scott argued. "That much data would completely lock up the system."

"Exponential fractal compression." The Legion agent took one last look at the screen, then turned to face Scott. "Think of it this way: If all the organizations were to build their own network for telecommunications, it might be rather obvious. By using the existing systems, we can piggyback our information on top of everyone else's."

Scott was starting to feel a little dizzy. In the space of a few hours he had learned that the one person he thought of as family was actually the creation of a bunch of mad scientists. Now he was faced with the idea that the computer systems he had been using all his life were just pieces of some vast unseen communications network run by people who wanted to take over the world.

Once again Scott wondered if he had done the right thing by letting Rhinehardt come along with him. The Legion agent might help him find Chloe, but Scott was sure the man had some definite ideas about what to do with Chloe once she had been found.

He thought for a moment about forcing the man to leave, but he couldn't bring himself to do it. If the Legion agent really could help locate Chloe, it was worth the risk. Any risk.

"What happens now?" Scott asked.

Rhinehardt got up from the chair and walked over to where he had left his small suitcase sitting on the floor. "Now we add my system to yours," he said. He knelt down beside the bag and flipped open the latches at the top. The sides of the bag fell open.

It took a few seconds for the contents of the suitcase to make any sense to Scott. And when he realized what he was seeing, his stomach leaped into his throat. "That's a *brain!*" he croaked.

"More than one, actually," Rhinehardt told Scott calmly. He reached into the case and pulled out the contents.

Inside a soft, translucent bag was a mass of convoluted, grayish pink tissue that sagged across the Legion agent's arms. Surrounding this central mass was a cloudy soup of yellow fluid that contained an assortment of lumps and blobs ranging from the size of a pea to the size of a golf ball.

Scott clamped a hand over his mouth. "That can't be a computer," he said through his fingers.

"A very effective computer," replied Rhinehardt. He carried the sloshing mass over to the counter and laid it beside the keyboard. The clear bag spread out over the Formica countertop, leaving the whole thing looking like a five-pound mass of spoiled hamburger under plastic wrap.

"But that's just a lump of meat!"

"It's a neurological calculating unit," said Rhinehardt. "Over thirty trillion cells, with more than a thousand cross connections each and a total storage equivalent to six yotabytes."

Scott wrinkled his nose and stepped closer to the mass of tissue. Enclosed in its plastic bag, the tissue seemed to quiver and pulsate. Scott felt his intestines twist a little tighter. "Is it really a brain?" he asked.

"Not now." The Legion agent rested a loving hand on the lump of pulsing flesh. "This system was bred from sheets of modified cortical cells grown around a complex form meant to optimize surface area."

"Yeah," said Scott. "Okay." He crept closer. The thing in the bag actually seemed to be swaying and twitching. He was willing to put that down to the sloshing of the fluid inside the plastic, but some of the smaller pieces were definitely moving around in the soup. "What are those swimming things?"

"Guppies," replied the Legion agent.

"You have fish in your computer?"

"Of course they've also been modified from their original form," Rhinehardt said. "They're designed to consume the excess lipoproteins that are given off during maximum synaptical stimulation."

"Of course," said Scott. "The lipoproteins." He felt as if he had fallen into some kind of strange dream. Surely he would wake up in a moment and have a good laugh about computers that were made of big blobs of brains and squads of guppies. "How can you possibly make this thing talk to my computer?"

"We need an interface unit," Rhinehardt answered. He went back to the suitcase, reached in, and pulled out a device that looked like a serial cable on one end and a salad fork on the other.

Scott gaped at the contraption in horror. "You aren't really going to . . . I mean . . ."

The Legion agent crossed the room, raised the pointed end of the device, and plunged it squarely into the center of the brain-computer. The computer began to scream like a wounded animal. Pale yellow fluid leaked out around the tines of the fork and oozed in thin streams down the side of the bag.

This time Scott's stomach didn't just move into his throat, it made an effort to escape from his body. He turned and ran for the nearest bathroom. All the way down the hall he could hear the blob of artificial brain making its high warbling scream. One part of Scott's own mind wondered how the thing could make any noise. After all, it had no throat, no lungs, no vocal cords. How could it scream? He decided that he really didn't want to know.

It took five minutes before he felt well enough to try doing something as complex as standing up. He staggered across the large bathroom and faced himself in the mirror. The guy in the mirror looked pale, sick, and really, really confused.

"I think you've made a big mistake," Scott told his reflection. "Now what are you going to do about it?"

The reflection offered no advice.

Scott splashed some cold water over his face and stuck his head out into the hall. The brain-computer had fallen quiet. Scott took a deep breath and was about to return to the computer room when he heard a sharp buzz fill the house. For a moment he thought it was another sound from Rhinehardt's awful computer-in-a-bag. Then he realized that it was only one of the security sensors. He hurried out into the main hallway, flipped off the alarm, and checked the closed-circuit camera system.

Most of the small black-and-white screens were clear, but in one of them Scott could see the tiny image of a car coming up the long curving drive that led to the mansion—an old, ugly car.

He winced. "Not now," he muttered. Then he raced for the door. It wasn't that he didn't want to see Dee. Before running into Rhinehardt, he had been looking forward to calling her. But right now didn't seem like the best time to be chatting about a school dance.

Scott managed to reach the front of the mansion just as Dee pulled up. "Hi!" he called.

Dee climbed out of her battered car and hurried toward the front door. Immediately Scott knew that something was wrong. Dee was usually wearing a wide smile when she visited him, but this time her expression was somber. "Hi," she replied softly.

"What's wrong?" Scott asked. "Is everybody okay?"

"Yeah." Dee nodded for a moment, then stopped and bit her lip. "At least everyone is okay for now. But I'm not sure how long that's going to last."

"Why? What's happened?"

Dee looked down at the ground. "My father says I'm not supposed to see you anymore."

Scott frowned. He had only met Dee's father a couple of times, but the man had seemed friendly enough. "I thought he liked me. What made him change his mind? Did I do something wrong?"

"No." Dee shook her head. "It's not you. It's Harley."

"I don't understand. How could your father be mad at *me* about something that *Harley* did?"

Dee frowned. "It's hard to explain," she said. "We need to go inside and talk."

Without thinking, Scott nodded. "Sure, come on—"

At that moment a sharp, rippling cry drifted down the stairs. Scott quickly jumped out of the house and shut the door.

Dee regarded him with a puzzled expression. "Aren't we going inside?"

"Uh . . ." Scott glanced over his shoulder and licked his lips nervously. "Maybe we should just talk out here."

The expression on Dee's face immediately turned to suspicion. "Why?" she asked. "The mosquitoes are biting me out here. Let's go inside."

The scream from the computer came again. This time it was loud enough that Scott could even hear it through the door. He stepped forward and put his hands on Dee's shoulders and turned her away from the house. "This isn't really a good time."

"Scott!" Dee protested. "This is important. We really need to talk."

Scott steered her gently—but quickly—back toward her car. "We'll talk," he promised. "I'll, uh . . . give you a call later tonight."

"But—"

The scream came again.

This time Scott could feel the muscles of Dee's shoulders grow tense under his hands. She stopped in her tracks. "What was *that*?"

"What was what?" Scott replied innocently.

"That noise." Dee pulled free of his grip and turned to squint at the house. "I heard something inside."

Scott glanced at the house, then at Dee. "I'm sure it

was just the security system," he improvised. "You know how Kenyon is—alarm, alarm, alarm."

Dee's eyes narrowed. "Kenyon is in Chicago, right?"

"Right."

"Then what set off the alarm? Is someone in the house?" asked Dee.

Scott's eyes widened. He could imagine what Dee would say if she saw the thing that was lying on the counter in the computer room. What he *couldn't* imagine was how he would explain to her how the brain-thing came to be in the house or why he was letting a Legion agent use their computer.

"No," he replied. He did his best to force a smile onto his lips. "Nobody here but me," he said. "It's just that, well . . . I'm in the middle of a big experiment right now. It's, um . . . very delicate. And if I don't go up there and take care of it, I'll have to start all over."

"I see," Dee said coldly. Her gaze swept up and down Scott's long frame. "I guess this experiment has something to do with finding Chloe."

"That's right." Scott nodded enthusiastically. "I'm looking for Chloe and it's really delicate and it would be better if you could . . . that is, if you would just . . ." Scott's voice trailed away. The expression on Dee's face told him that he had made a mistake. A big mistake.

Over a period of a second Dee's face grew almost as dark as her auburn hair. "I see," she repeated in a brittle voice. "Your search for Chloe is more important than your relationship with me."

"Yes . . . I mean, *no.*" Scott shook his head. "Of course not. It's just that this is a critical time."

"I'll say it's a critical time," Dee replied sharply. "I tell you my father never wants me to see you again and all you can do is shove me away!"

"That's not what I'm trying to—" Scott began.

Another scream came from inside the house, followed by a burst of a strange gurgling noise.

Dee stepped past him. "You're going to tell me *that* was an alarm?"

"Sure." Scott hurried to get between Dee and the front door. "Kenyon has some very unusual systems installed."

"I'll bet." Dee stood still for a moment, then gave a sharp nod. "All right," she said. "I'm going."

Scott breathed a sigh of relief. He walked behind Dee as she went back to her car and opened the driver's-side door. He leaned down as she climbed into the car. "We'll talk later, okay?"

Dee pulled the door shut and glanced at Scott through the open window. "I don't think there's any need to talk. It's obvious that you care more about someone you lost five years ago than the one you're losing right now."

Scott felt a sick feeling that was far worse than the illness that had come over him when he looked at the brain-computer. "Dee . . ."

Before he could think of anything else to say, Dee closed the door, cranked the car, and roared away with a squeal of rubber and a puff of blue smoke. Scott watched the angular taillights of the old Gremlin disappear around the sweep of the driveway, then turned reluctantly toward the house.

He couldn't believe that Dee was serious about not seeing him again. He liked Dee. He thought, maybe, that he even loved her. But Scott had grown up in institutions, and there had been very few examples of love in his life. He had never had any family—unless Chloe counted. Dee was his first real girlfriend. He didn't know how people in love were supposed to act.

There was no sound from the brain-computer as Scott climbed the stairs to the computer room, but the scene in the room made him freeze. Gunter Rhinehardt sat hunched over the keyboard. Beside him the brain in its plastic bag was swollen and misshapen. The folds of tissue that had been a pale pink-gray were now puffy and as dark purple as a bruise. The metal fork of the connection device trembled in the center of this mass, and a trickle of yellow fluid dripped into a puddle on the tile floor. All around the brain the pale forms of the modified guppies circled madly—like sharks that had scented blood.

Scott stayed near the door, unwilling to go closer. "Does it have to scream?" he asked.

"It doesn't," Rhinehardt said without turning. "The sounds you hear are produced by nothing more than sympathetic vibrations of the interface equipment. The neurological system is not capable of feeling pain."

Scott looked at the swollen purple thing in the bag. He had an idea that the awful creation might experience a lot more pain than its creators were willing to admit. "It looks sick."

"The data you have collected contains a rich association of information," said Rhinehardt. "The sheer volume is placing a strain on the system."

"Are you finding anything?" Scott asked.

Rhinehardt spun around in the chair. "Oh yes," he said. "In fact, I believe I have already located Chloe Adair."

SIX

There was such a thing as too quiet.

Harley flipped over on her side in the bed. No matter which way she turned, the sheets tangled around her long legs and some lump in the pillow found its way under her head. Finally she gave up, climbed out of the bed, and walked over to the window.

The rain and clouds that had obscured the sky earlier in the day had completely vanished, leaving a brilliant moon sailing across a velvet night. Harley grabbed the handle at the side of the window and cranked open the glass. At once the room was filled with the soft rhythm of the waves breaking against the shore. In the distance was the rougher sound of the water striking the high bluffs north of Stone Harbor.

Harley closed her eyes and smiled. It was April, and the night air was still chilly, but Harley was more than willing to suffer a little chill in exchange for the rushing noise of water on sand. Despite all the places she had lived while traveling with her father, Harley had never been on the ocean before she came to Stone Harbor. After a month at the beach house she found it hard to believe she could live anywhere else.

She returned to the bed, untwisted the tangled sheets, and lay down. Almost instantly the warm darkness expanded, ready to carry her away from the confusing, frightening day. But before the darkness could swallow her troubled thoughts, a light appeared.

Harley smiled. "Noah," she whispered against her pillow.

Since he had vanished into the white sphere, Noah had appeared to her only in dreams or visions. Harley hadn't been visited by one of the dreams since she'd returned to Stone Harbor, and she had begun to fear she would never have another.

The light swelled and took on a mixture of tones— golden sunlight, grass green. Harley felt a moment of dizziness, and she found herself standing in the middle of a field surrounded by waist-high grass and a riot of pale blooms. The red sun hung over the top of distant trees, and the air was full of the sweet, bakery smell of ripe grain.

A shadow passed over Harley. She looked up in time to see a red-tailed hawk streaking across an impossibly blue sky.

Harley waved up at the bird. "Tell Noah I'm here!" she called. The bird gave her a glance with a gold-ringed eye, then screeched and beat its wide wings. In a moment it was gone.

Harley looked around her for a landmark, but she could see nothing that looked familiar from her previous visits. "Noah!" she shouted hopefully.

Almost at once there was a shout of reply from a patch of tall grass ahead.

Harley felt her heart jump as Noah Templer emerged from the stalks and walked toward her across the field.

Noah bore little resemblance to the high-school student Harley had met when she arrived in Stone Harbor. He wore no shirt, and the sun of the dream world had tanned his broad shoulders almost as dark as his leather belt. The tan outlined the new muscles of Noah's chest and arms. Instead of the jeans he had worn when he stepped into the sphere, he now wore pants of a rough, bark-colored home-spun cloth. His wavy blond hair, which had been cut short before he disappeared, was long enough to spill almost to his shoulders.

Noah raised a hand as he drew near. "I'm glad to see you," he called. "I was afraid you weren't coming."

Harley laughed. *"You* were afraid!" She ran to close the distance between them and threw her arms around Noah. She pressed her face against his chest and closed her eyes. He was here, he was solid. "I was starting to wonder if I'd ever see you again."

"Has it been that long?" Noah asked softly. He had warned Harley before that time inside the sphere and outside didn't always move at the same pace.

"It's been weeks," she said. "Why haven't you let me in?"

Noah's arms slipped around Harley's shoulders, and he gave her a firm hug. "I don't let you in," he said. "It takes both of us working together to bring you here. And the conditions aren't always right. It's like . . . weather."

"Well, I hope the weather stays good for a long time," said Harley. "I want to come in and see you every day."

"I'm not sure that's a good idea," Noah replied.

Harley opened her eyes and looked up to see that there was an expression of concern on Noah's face. "What's wrong?" she asked.

He frowned and glanced over his shoulder for a moment. "I think it may be dangerous for you to be here," he said. "There are . . . others . . . in here who aren't so friendly."

"What are you talking about?" Harley asked. "I've never seen anyone here but you. Besides, I thought you *made* this place."

The last time Harley had visited this dream world, Noah had said that the whole place was really only a construction—an artificial world held within his mind. To Harley the idea seemed incredible. It was true that the first time she had come to Noah's world, the place had seemed a little sketchy, but with every visit since then the place had seemed bigger, more detailed. More real. But there was far too much to the place for it to all be just one person's imagination. If Noah really had the ability to create such things with nothing but his thoughts, Harley didn't even want to guess at what else he might be able to do.

"I did create this place," Noah replied. "Or at least what you've seen of it. But the longer it's here, the more of the others it seems to draw. They're like moths coming to a light in the darkness. I can't keep them away forever."

"Them? Who are you talking about? Did some more people get trapped inside the sphere?"

"I'm not sure," Noah replied slowly. "I think . . ."

He shook his head. "I'm not even sure that all of them are human."

Harley felt a chill. She stepped away from Noah and wrapped her arms around herself. "If they're not human, then what are they?"

Noah reached out and brushed her dark hair away from her face. "I wish I could explain," he said. "I don't even know where to start. You'll just have to trust me when I say that this place is getting too dangerous to come for a visit."

Harley shook her head. "I have to come," she said. She stared into Noah's sunburned face. "I have to see you."

For a moment Noah smiled. "Oh, I think you'll be seeing me." His smile faded, and he glanced over his shoulder again. "But today I think there's someone else you need to see."

"What?"

"I think there's at least one person here you'll want to see," Noah explained patiently.

At once Harley's heart skipped a beat. "It's my dad," she said. "Isn't it?" Her father had disappeared into the sphere along with Noah, but there had never been any sign of him in the dream world. Harley stepped past Noah and peered into the tall grass. "Dad!" she called in excitement. "Dad! Are you out there? Dad! It's Harley!"

There was no reply.

"Where is he?" asked Harley. "Where is my fa—" Her voice died in her throat as she realized she was alone. Noah Templer was gone. "Noah?" Harley called. Her throat had suddenly become choked, and she had a hard time squeezing out his name. "Noah, are you there?" She turned around and around in the grass, but there was nothing. There wasn't even a bent stalk to show where Noah had been.

Harley waited for several minutes, but Noah didn't return or respond to her calls. Finally she began to walk toward the trees at the end of the field. They didn't look any more familiar than anything else, but at least they were a destination.

A breeze rippled through the grass, and a cluster of pale yellow moths headed for the sky at Harley's approach. Harley smiled nervously at them as they flittered away. She pushed on through the field. As she walked, the grass around her grew higher and higher. Soon the top of the grass was well above her head and Harley was lost in a miniature forest of brown and green stalks.

For the first time in the dreamland she felt a tickle of fear. Something about the place felt different. On her previous visits it had been warm, green, rich, and lovely. It was still beautiful, but there was a sense of some vast, distant shadow hanging over this inner world—something that made the world seem sadder than it had before.

Harley drew in a deep breath of cool air. Back in Stone Harbor it was officially spring, though the nights were still chilly with the last traces of winter. But in this place the air had the crisp, dusty edge of autumn. It seemed to promise pumpkins and corn shucks and Halloween just around the corner.

The dreamland had grown colder. Drier. Deader.

She pushed forward more quickly, leaving a trail of

broken stalks in her wake and accumulating a dusting of grass seeds in her hair. Her fear was growing. If this world had changed so much, it might mean something was wrong with Noah.

Harley heard movement in the tall grass.

She froze. "Noah?" she asked. She spoke so softly that his name was little more than a sigh.

Whoever—whatever—was in the field, it was getting closer. There was a soft, hissing sound as the stalks of grass were pushed apart. Ripples ran through the field like waves crossing a still pool.

Dream or not, Harley could feel her heart pounding against her ribs as she stood paralyzed. Something was coming, and she didn't think it was Noah Templer.

The sound drew closer. Closer. Then a glimmer of white appeared through the brown grass.

A woman walked across the field. She was a tall, thin woman with waves of dark hair and high cheekbones in a slender heart-shaped face. She was dressed all in white, a long flowing gown that swept out behind her and brushed against the grass. The woman passed so close that Harley could have reached out and touched her, but Harley's arms only hung stiffly at her sides, as frozen as the rest of her.

The figure in white floated past, moving through the field with a slow, stately grace. Her dark eyes were focused on some distant point. She didn't even turn her head to look in Harley's direction as she went by. The white dress was lost behind a screen of grass. The sound of the woman's passage faded and disappeared.

Harley's paralysis ended as quickly as if someone had thrown a switch. She turned to face the silent grass. "Wait!" she called. She took a few hurried steps in the direction the woman had disappeared. Harley's own passage through the grass had left a trail of broken and trampled stalks, but the woman in white had left no trace of her existence.

"Wait!" Harley shouted again. "I'm here!" A tear rolled down her cheek and dropped into the dry grass. "Mother!" she cried. "Come back!"

Then the sun went out.

There was a moment of horrible dizziness and disorientation before Harley realized that she was back in her bed at the beach house, with the muted rumble of waves breaking on the beach. She sat up in the darkness and ran her hands through her hair.

All her life Harley had believed—had known—that her mother had died when she was just a kid. One of her earliest memories was of the rainy day when she had stood next to her father and watched a pine coffin lowered into the ground. But when her father disappeared, Harley had found clues to a different history.

Her father's journals described a series of experiments. Harley couldn't be certain, but it seemed that those experiments involved using her mother to produce some new kind of mental energy—the same energy used to power the white sphere.

And then Harley had seen the woman in the tube.

In a secret Unit 17 medical facility hidden within a New Jersey office park, Harley had come across a room crowded with an incredible array of high-tech equipment. In the center of the room, held within a tube of liquid, was a woman. Harley had been captured and tortured before she had a chance to learn more, but she had good reason to suspect that woman was her mother.

In the dark beach house Harley stared at the wall and tried to recall her mother's face. Once she had kept her mother's picture next to her bed, but Unit 17 had taken all her personal belongings months before. Harley had nothing left of her mother, her father, or her life but her memories.

Harley took a deep breath of the cold air rolling in off the ocean. Her memories of her mother had been washed away by time. She couldn't say for sure that the woman in the tube had really been her mother. In fact, it seemed almost impossible. But with everything that had happened to her in the past few months, even the impossible didn't seem . . . impossible.

The dusty remains of the strange dream scattered in Harley's mind. She fell back against the sweat-soaked sheets and closed her eyes. In a few moments exhaustion began to overcome her fear. But before sleep could close around her, Harley heard the sound of a car easing slowly down the gravel drive toward the beach house.

Tired as she was, Harley got up quickly and picked up her blue jeans from the chair beside the bed. Whoever was outside, she didn't want them to catch her half dressed. Without turning on the lights, she slipped on her jeans and fumbled on the ground for her sneakers. By the time she heard a car door open and close, Harley was ready.

Footsteps crunched toward the door. Harley tiptoed into the living room and crouched behind a chair. The person at the door might be NSA agent Morris, or Lydia Abel, or anyone else. It seemed to Harley that her secret hideaway was turning into Grand Central station.

The screen door opened with a squeak, and the doorknob rattled. "Harley," called a loud whisper from outside. "Harley, are you up?"

Harley opened the door to reveal Dee Janes standing on the small porch. "Isn't it kind of late?"

Dee pushed past her into the dark living room. "Had to be. I'd already gotten in trouble for going out to visit Scott. I couldn't sneak over here until my dad was asleep."

Harley eased the door closed. "And was something so important that you had to come over here at midnight?"

"Actually," Dee replied, "it's closer to two."

Just hearing the time made Harley's mouth stretch open in a yawn. She snapped on the light switch and squinted against the sudden brightness. "What's up?" she asked. "Why wouldn't your dad let you out?"

"Typical stuff," said Dee. She walked across the room, dropped onto the couch, and leaned back. "Somebody's out to kill you."

Harley sighed. She sat down on the chair facing the couch. "Anybody new?"

Dee shrugged. "It's hard to tell. Dad got more

'wanted' announcements at the station today." She wrinkled her nose. "Very bad pictures of you."

"That figures." Harley pushed her hair back from her face and covered another yawn. At the moment she felt so worn-out and exhausted that it didn't seem possible for there to be a *good* picture that featured her. "But why would your dad be upset by that?" she asked. "He gets those things all the time."

"This one had your name on it," said Dee. "Your new name, I mean. It seems that Kathleen Vincent is now wanted just as much as Kathleen Davisidaro. Suspect in a murder investigation."

Harley winced. Unit 17 had used false police reports to try to smoke her out, but the charges had never included murder. And they had never known about the false name Cain had provided. "It seems like somebody is getting serious."

"I don't know," said Dee. "If they know all about your false ID, it seems like they should be able to find you pretty easily."

Maybe they already have, Harley thought. Both Abel and the NSA had found her in the same day. She wondered if either of them had been responsible for the new police reports. "Does your dad have any idea what to do now?"

Dee frowned and stared down at the floor. "Only that he thinks it's getting too dangerous for me to be around you. He said, well . . . he *ordered* me to stay away. He wants me to stay away from you and away from Scott and Kenyon."

Harley nodded but couldn't think of anything to say. Dee was the best friend she had, but Dee's father was right—being close to Harley really *was* dangerous.

Dee glanced up and smiled weakly. "You know what I think? I think we need to find another place for you to stay before someone shows up to see you."

Harley thought for a moment of mentioning the two strangers who had come to meet her that day and decided against it. Despite Dee's joking manner, Harley could tell that she was already upset. But considering all the company in Stone Harbor, moving out of the beach house didn't seem like a bad idea. "Where could I go?" she asked. "Kenyon has already paid out for this place. Noah's house is gone. The little place on the lake is a wreck, and it sounds like your dad is not going to exactly welcome me back into your house with open arms."

"There is a place," said Dee. She leaned forward. "You could stay up at the mansion with Scott and Kenyon."

Harley scowled. "I don't think that's such a good idea."

"Come on," Dee insisted. "There must be a dozen bedrooms in that place. It's not like I'm asking you to share a room with Kenyon."

"I still don't think it's such a good idea. Kenyon and I, well, we're . . ."

Harley's voice trailed away as she thought about Kenyon. At one time Harley would have said she could barely tolerate the handsome rich kid who spent millions the way most people used pocket change. Then she and Kenyon had endured a terrible trip across the country and had each thought the other one dead. That time had changed things between them. It was clear, even to Harley, that Kenyon cared for her more than he was willing to admit. And Harley's feelings for Kenyon were . . . confused.

Dee pressed her lips together and reached out to touch Harley on the arm. "There's another reason I want you to move to the mansion," she said.

Harley frowned in puzzlement. "What?"

"It's Scott. I want you to watch out for him."

"Is he okay?"

"Yeah." Dee nodded for a moment, then stopped. "At least I *think* he's okay."

"Then why do you want me to watch out for him?"

Dee shrugged. "I was out there earlier. Scott was acting really strange."

"Scott *always* acts strange," replied Harley.

"*Stranger,*" said Dee. "I needed to talk to him, and he practically pushed me away from the place."

Harley had to admit that did seem odd. Scott might spend most of his time with his nose against a computer monitor, but Scott and Dee had been an item almost from the moment they met. "Did he say why?"

Dee nodded. "Something about finding Chloe. But he's always trying to find Chloe. I think something else is going on."

"Something like what?"

"I don't know," Dee admitted. "But something."

Harley thought for a moment, then nodded. "All right," she said. "I'll see about getting out there to see him tomorrow."

Dee's face lit up in a wide grin. "Cool." She stood up. "See you at school tomorrow?"

Harley hadn't even thought about going back to school. After her meeting with the NSA agent, six hours of algebra and PE didn't seem to make much sense. But she didn't have anything else to do besides sit around somewhere and jump at shadows. "Sure," she said. "I guess."

Dee gave her a quick hug. "Okay." She grinned again. "Don't stay up too late."

Harley followed her friend to the door and watched as Dee started her battered car. She stood in the doorway for a moment, breathing in the night air, and was just about to close the door when something caught her eye.

Down on the beach a pale figure was walking in the moonlight.

For the space of a heartbeat Harley froze. Then she sprinted out of the house.

"Hey!" she shouted. "Hold on!"

Saw grass whipped against her legs as she ran across the low dunes separating the small house from the sea. With each step the figure on the beach became clearer. It was a woman, a woman with dark hair and a long white gown. She was walking along the tide line with water swirling around her ankles.

"Wait!" Harley called. "Mother!"

The woman in white was *there*, right in front of her.

And then, with the very next step, the woman vanished. Only a patch of white foam riding on the waves remained.

Harley stumbled and splashed to a stop. "Mom? Mother!"

She received no answer. But between one wave and the next she could have sworn she saw a line of footsteps in the damp sand.

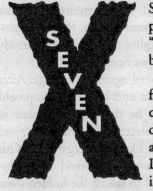

SEVEN

Scott turned the sheet of paper over in his hands. "What is *this* supposed to be?" he asked.

Rhinehardt looked up from his breakfast. "That's a cladistical analysis of the data transepts," he replied around a bite of toast. The Legion agent and his screaming brain-PC had worked so late that Scott had fallen asleep in his chair. The long hours seemed to have given the former guard a healthy appetite—he was already on his second plate of eggs and shoving down toast almost as fast as it could be toasted.

"Cladistical?" asked Scott.

Rhinehardt reached out and tapped the paper, leaving a greasy smudge on the white page. "This compiles a relationship image of the various messages by examining points of similarity," he explained. "It's based on a system that helps to determine family trees among extinct mammals."

"Okay. Extinct mammal trees." Scott looked at the paper. To him it appeared to be meaningless sets of letters and numbers that were grouped together in lumpy clusters and connected by lines of different widths. If there was any plan to the thing—or a single word of English—he couldn't find it. "And this is what you're using to locate Chloe?"

The Legion agent nodded. "It's primarily an analysis of the data already stored in your system. From the density of these patterns, I'm quite certain that it already contains all the information we need."

"That's good." Scott looked again at the page. After years of sorting through data and building equipment in an effort to find Chloe, he thought of himself as something of an expert on electronics, computers, and data encryption. Now he felt like a kindergartner on his first day. He couldn't begin to understand the brain-computer, the system it used to search for hidden data, or even the report that Rhinehardt had produced. He scanned the paper one last time, then tossed the meaningless page onto the kitchen table. "All right," he said. "Where's Chloe?"

Gunter Rhinehardt put down his fork and carefully wiped his lips with a napkin before answering. "I don't know."

"What? But you said—"

The Legion agent silenced Scott with an upraised hand. "I said we had all the information we needed," he stated calmly. "I didn't say I had finished the analysis required to determine Ms. Adair's actual location."

"All right," said Scott. "So how long will it take you and your sack of spare brains to figure it out?"

Rhinehardt shook his head. "The system I have here is insufficient to the task."

"What does that mean?" Scott asked with a frown.

The Legion agent pushed his chair back from the table and stood. "It means I need to take the neurological unit and the information it has gathered to a place where it can be directly interfaced with a more powerful unit."

It took a moment before Scott got the meaning of the man's words. When he did, he stood up quickly. "You mean you're *leaving?*"

"Yes." Rhinehardt nodded. "Once I join the portable unit to one of our large mass arrays, we should have the source of this data pinpointed in a matter of moments."

Scott shook his head. "No," he said. "No way."

"I don't understand," replied the former guard. "I thought you *wanted* me to find Ms. Adair."

"I do." Scott picked up the incomprehensible report from the table and waved it. "I want to find Chloe more than anything in the world, but there's no way I can let you come in here, read all the data I've collected, and then run off with the information."

"I see." The Legion agent's face went cold. For a moment he looked all too much like the stern orphanage worker who Scott remembered from his childhood.

"But you already have let me into your home, and I have already examined your data—in far greater detail than you would ever manage on your own." He reached across the table and pulled the report from Scott's hand. "What would you have me do?" he asked. "Destroy my system and forget what I have learned? What did you think I came to do?"

"To . . . find Chloe," Scott said weakly. The truth was that he hadn't really thought about what Rhinehardt might do. Somewhere inside he had to have known that the man would eventually take what he had learned and leave. But the Legion agent had offered a chance to find Chloe, and for that chance Scott had put aside his fears, suspicions, and common sense.

"And to find her, I must return to our primary analysis center," said Rhinehardt.

Scott frowned. "But why can't you do it from here?" he asked. There was a note of whining in his voice that sounded childish even to himself, but he couldn't help it. "You said you can transmit all this data over the Internet. So why don't you use that to talk to your bigger brain?"

Rhinehardt only shook his head. "No. That's not possible. The data has to go with me."

"I see." Scott wasn't the kind of person who got angry very often, but as he looked across the table at the Legion agent he felt a rising sense of betrayal. "I'm not letting you out of here with that information. You might leave and never come back."

"That is possible." The former guard lifted a glass from the table and drained the last of his orange juice. He set it down on the wood with a solid thump. "But I would advise you never to make a statement that might be interpreted as a threat."

Scott shrugged. "Take it however you want to take it, but that data stays here."

The words were barely out of his mouth when he felt a tingling all over his skin. Across the room a line of copper pots began to rattle against the wall.

The oven door flopped open with a clang. The

lights above the kitchen table flared so bright that Scott cringed, then they faded to a dull, sullen glow.

"If you are going to make threats," said Rhinehardt, "then you better be very sure that you can carry them out."

A thump of something falling echoed in another part of the house, and one of the security sensors began to emit a series of short, erratic bleeps, as if the device wasn't quite sure there was something wrong. "Are *you* doing this?" Scott demanded. "What's going on?"

Rhinehardt didn't answer, but he didn't need to. Outside the picture window on the other side of the kitchen a sphere of red light rose into view. It was small, a little larger than a basketball, and it glowed like the heart of a campfire. Even seen against the morning light outside, the sphere seemed so thick with light that it was almost solid.

Scott's mouth dropped open. Harley had described such spheres to him, but he had never seen one. Until that moment he had believed they were only part of Harley's dreams, like her "visits" from Noah, but the thing outside the kitchen window was all too real. "What *is* that?"

"A courier," Rhinehardt replied. "Also a guardian and an assistant. It bows to my will and enforces my commands."

The sphere rose a foot higher in the air. Slowly it contracted until it was a brilliant circle of light no bigger than a softball. The kitchen window began to melt. The frame didn't burn, and the wall around the window seemed unharmed, but the glass itself was definitely glowing, softening, and flowing like cold syrup. The window glass thickened at the bottom and thinned out in the center. For a moment it was as thin as a soap bubble in the middle, reflecting a distorted image of the room. Then the bubble popped, leaving a hole the size of a quarter. Quickly the hole expanded to the size of a silver dollar, then to the width of a saucer, then to the diameter of a dinner plate. Streamers of liquid glass drizzled from the edge of the window frame and gathered in smoking puddles on the hardwood floors.

The bright red sphere passed through the opening. Once inside, it swelled back to basketball size and hovered in the air next to the ruined window.

"You see," said Rhinehardt. "You are in no position to be making threats."

Scott kept his eye on the floating ball of light. "What powers these things?" he asked. "Is it transmitted energy?"

To his surprise, Rhinehardt laughed. "Always the technologist," he said. "Even as a child you couldn't resist an engineering challenge. It was you who figured out how to open the locks at the orphanage, wasn't it?"

"Yes." Scott felt a twinge of guilt. Every time he thought about that night, he wondered what would have happened if he had never learned to pick the locks. Chloe might have tried to escape the Benevolence Home in another way, but she might not have been captured by the dark forces at work in the access tunnel.

"A love for technology is good," said Rhinehardt. "It's one of the things we encourage within Legion and one of the reasons we have advanced so very far." He reached into the pocket of his pants and came out with a small object. "For instance, take a look at this."

Scott leaned forward and squinted. As far as he could tell, the object was nothing but a piece of bent metal, something like a small horseshoe. "What is—" he began.

Then the world went away.

It was like falling into a television that was caught between channels. Gray, trembling mist covered Scott's vision in all directions, and a hiss filled his ears.

He tried to reach out, but there was no sense of motion or touch. He tried to shout, but there was no sound. There was no sense of left or right, no weight, no heat or cold. No pain. Nothing but the endless, senseless static.

To Scott the time in the gray nothing might have been minutes, hours, or days. He had no way to tell. He couldn't even feel himself breathing. He thought that he should have been terrified—whatever the Legion agent had done to him might be permanent. He might be caught in a coma forever. He might be dead. But even fear was beyond him. His emotions were as cut off as his senses.

Finally, after some unknown length of time, shapes began to form out of the grayness. The shadowy forms gradually gained color and detail. A wall. The edge of a counter. A white plate lying broken on a hardwood floor.

Scott realized he was lying sprawled in the middle of

the kitchen. It took a few more minutes for the paralysis to leave his limbs and a minute after that before he was able to sit up and rub his head.

He had felt no pain while in the gray static, but now that he was free, Scott felt as if his head were going to split open. A sharp, pulsing pain throbbed behind his eyes, ran across his head, and reached down his neck. Trembling, he put his hand on the edge of the table and stood.

Rhinehardt and the red sphere were gone. Only the hole that had been welded through the center of the window remained.

It's going to be fun explaining *that* to Kenyon, Scott thought.

A strange whistling noise came from outside. Scott stumbled to the window in time to see a strange craft descend from the sky. The aircraft was small, no bigger than a go-cart, with a single seat caught in a frame of thin carbon-fiber tubes. Above the seat *something* stirred in the air. It didn't seem to be a helicopter blade. In fact, it didn't seem to be anything solid at all. There was only a patch of air that jittered and rippled like the space above a black highway on a hot summer day.

Whatever the shimmering space was, it was obvious that the craft could fly. It settled onto the driveway outside as easily as a feather touching down. The single seat was empty.

A moment later Scott saw Gunter Rhinehardt step into view. The Legion agent held a sheaf of printer data in one hand and the handle of his cheap suitcase in the other. Behind him the red sphere floated in the air like a dog trailing after its master.

Scott clenched his teeth in determination. He wasn't going to let the data get away without putting up some fight.

Still shaken from the effects of Rhinehardt's weapon, he ran into the hallway and threw open a dark wooden cabinet. Inside he found a dizzying array of weapons, from fully automatic rifles to a collection of handguns. Scott had never fired a gun in his life, but he pulled a pump shotgun from the center of the lineup and hurried outside.

Rhinehardt was still climbing into his strange aircraft when Scott came running up. "Hold it right there!" Scott shouted. "You're going nowhere!"

As fast as a bullet the red sphere zipped around Rhinehardt and hovered between Scott and the Legion agent. The ball of light pulsed and throbbed in a way that made it look almost angry.

"Be very careful," Rhinehardt cautioned. "If the sphere believes I'm being threatened, it may act without my command."

"Get out of the machine," Scott ordered. "Bring the brain back inside."

"I can't do that." Rhinehardt settled into the seat and pulled a bar down across his chest. "I must locate Chloe Adair. Let me go, and the central neurocomputer systems will process this information in no more than an hour. I'll be back before noon."

Scott tried to ignore the ball of light hovering no

more than a dozen feet away. He leveled the shotgun and pointed it toward Rhinehardt. "I want to find Chloe, too," he said. "But I can't let you leave. Come inside and we'll talk about it."

To his surprise, the Legion agent smiled. "I don't believe you'll shoot me."

"You'd *better* believe it," Scott replied grimly. He lowered his eye to the gun sight. The weapon's metal barrel felt cold against his cheek. "Get out of that machine. Now."

"No," said Rhinehardt.

Scott blinked sweat away from his eye. "I'll do it," he warned.

"No," the Legion agent said calmly. "You won't."

For the space of ten heartbeats Scott kept the gun sight centered on the man. Then he slowly lowered the weapon. "How can you be so sure?" he asked.

"Because," Rhinehardt replied, "it wasn't only Chloe who I was watching at the Benevolence Home."

The patch of rippling air above the Legion agent's seat grew wider. With only a faint hum the chair rose into the air, turned, and sailed off into the clouds. For a second the red sphere remained, hovering in front of Scott like a hummingbird examining a flower. Then the ball of light bobbed up and down once, performed a neat loop, and zipped away.

EIGHT

"Ms. Janes," asked the science teacher, "are you supposed to be in this class?"

"Um, not exactly," Dee admitted. She took a step into the classroom. "I was just looking for Har . . . I mean for Kathleen Vincent."

The teacher nodded. "Well, Ms. Vincent has not seen fit to grace us with her presence so far today. Why don't you go and try paying a visit to your own classroom? Maybe she's looking for you there."

The snickers of two dozen students followed Dee out the door. She walked a few yards down the hallway, stopped, and leaned against the lockers. As far as she could tell, Harley hadn't been in school all day. Dee knew it was possible that Harley had simply decided to blow off the day, but with only a couple of weeks left in the year and finals looming, Harley had been having a hard time getting ready. Considering the posters that had come through the police department, Dee feared that Harley's reason for missing class might be far more serious.

"Hey, do you have a hall pass?"

Dee turned and saw Jilly Wickman walking toward her. Jilly was skinny and had braces so big and complex, they looked like a scale model for a new suspension bridge. She was also the most notorious teacher's pet in the school.

"Go away, Jilly."

"I'm the hall monitor," the skinny girl replied. "You can't tell me what to do."

"Yeah?" Dee turned. "Look, Jilly—" She broke off. Dee had been within a breath of delivering a comment on what she thought of Jilly's abilities as a hall monitor, as a human being, and as a waste of precious metal resources. But at the last moment she decided that spending the morning in the principal's office was not an effective way to help Harley. "Look," she began again. "I'm really sorry. I just forgot something, okay?"

Jilly smirked in response. "That doesn't matter," she said. "I'm going to have to write you up."

Dee swallowed her anger and actually smiled. "Sure," she said. "I guess you have to." *You pathetic tin-mouthed twig.*

The lack of a good argument seemed to disappoint Jilly. She frowned and looked away. "Well," she said. "Maybe we can forget it this time."

"Thanks, Jilly," Dee said cheerfully. "You're really great." *You little weasel.*

Jilly turned and retreated down the corridor.

Dee stood in the hall for a moment longer, then reached a decision. Skipping a half a day of classes wasn't going to affect her grades that much. Checking on Harley was more important than spending another afternoon hearing about the social implications of Madame Bovary. She drew a deep breath and headed for the door to the parking lot.

She had taken no more than ten steps when she

heard a voice from behind her. "Do you have a hall pass?"

Dee gritted her teeth. "No," she said. "I don't have a hall pass." She started to turn around and face the beast of the hallway. "Jilly, I already—"

Only it wasn't Jilly. Instead Dee found herself face-to-face with a woman who she'd never seen before. "Who are *you?*"

The woman scowled. She had a severely beautiful face, with deep blue eyes set on either side of a long aristocratic nose and a cloud of dark curls surrounding her head. It was a very good face for scowling. "Is it the students who ask the questions in this school?" she asked. The woman had an accent to match the nose—very clipped, vaguely British, and rolled in money.

At first glance the woman looked barely old enough to be out of high school, but she carried herself with an air of absolute authority. Student teacher, thought Dee. Has to be. "Sorry. I thought you were someone else."

"Obviously." The woman raised her royal nose into the air and sniffed. "All right," she said. "Come with me." She spun on her heel and started back down the hallway.

Dee groaned. She was tempted to make a dash for it. After all, the woman probably didn't know her name. But after all the times Dee had made a little visit to the principal's office, she had no doubt that a description would be enough for a positive ID. She trudged down the hall after the teacher.

To Dee's surprise, the woman didn't lead her to the

principal's office. Instead she marched to a doorway halfway down the left side of the hall and jerked it open. "In here," she demanded.

As far as Dee knew, the room the woman had opened was only used for band practice. In the middle of the school day the room was silent and empty. Dee walked obediently inside and waited while the woman closed the door.

"What are we doing in here?" asked Dee, gesturing at the rows of music stands and folding chairs.

The woman pulled the shade down to cover the small window in the door, then turned toward Dee. "This is supposed to be a place of learning," she replied. "I thought it might be time you received a little education."

"What are you—"

A ringing sound clanged in Dee's ears and a jolt went through her from head to toe. She staggered back. A music stand toppled with a crash. Dee blinked a sudden flow of water from her eyes. It took her several seconds to put all these events into sequence and several more to find the right words for what had just happened. "You *hit* me," she gasped in astonishment.

The woman nodded. "I said I was going to provide some education. Consider that your first lesson."

Dee raised a hand and touched her burning cheek. "But teachers aren't allowed to hit students." The idea that she had actually been attacked was astonishing.

"Who said I was a teacher?" the woman replied. She took two steps forward, pulled back her hand, and delivered a blow that knocked Dee to the floor.

Dee lay on the dusty tiles and looked through the forest of music stands at the legs of the woman who was battering her. She felt dizzy, confused, angry, and just a little bit afraid. "Help!" she shouted. "Someone help!"

The toe of the woman's right shoe drove into Dee's side, forcing the air from her lungs and sending stars across her vision. "You can call all you want," the woman said. "This room was designed to shield the rest of the school from the sound of fifty off-key band students. I don't think anyone's going to hear you." The woman drew back her leg for another kick.

This time Dee rolled out of the way. She reached out and snatched the fallen music stand from the floor. Holding the clumsy weapon carefully in front of her, Dee climbed back to her feet. "You better stop that," she said in her best imitation of her father's tough cop voice.

The woman nodded. "Very good. You're learning already."

"Why did you hit me?" Dee demanded.

"I hit you because your friend Harley Davisidaro was not available to hit," the woman replied.

The little spark of fear in Dee's guts grew quickly. If the woman knew Harley and knew Harley's real name, then she had to be involved with one of the secret groups. "Where are you from? Umbra?"

The woman sneered. "Hardly." She turned away from Dee and walked slowly around the room. "My name is Lydia Abel. I represent the same organization that employed Ian Cain."

Dee studied the slender woman. She wore a sheer, silky blue dress that stopped well short of her knees. Her skin was a smooth tan, and there was something exotic in her features. The woman certainly didn't seem to have anything in common with the tall, dour Agent Cain in his consistently drab tan trench coat.

"Cain never acted like you," Dee observed.

Lydia Abel shrugged her bare shoulders. "Ian's behavior was his own affair."

"How do I know you work for the same people?"

The question drew a harsh laugh from the dark-haired woman. "If you're waiting for me to show you my identification, you're going to have a long wait." She paused, lifted a book of marching music from a stand, and thumbed idly through the pages. "This is something you will just have to accept on faith."

Right, thought Dee. Like the Easter bunny. "Cain and Abel," she said. "Someone at your organization has a sense of humor."

"Yes," the woman agreed, "but I can assure you it was not I who chose these names."

Dee glanced toward the door and tried to judge the distance. Unlike Harley, Dee wasn't a fast runner, but she still thought she could beat this woman to the door. Still holding the music stand in her hands, she edged toward the exit. "If you really work for the same people as Cain, then why would you want to hit Harley?"

Abel dropped the music book and looked across the room at Dee. "Because she's responsible for the death of a fine field agent."

"Cain?" Dee shook her head firmly. "Harley didn't kill Cain. Cain died saving her life. He saved all our lives."

"Exactly," replied Lydia Abel. She folded her arms below her chest. "Don't ever expect me to make that mistake. If it comes down to a choice between saving myself or saving the likes of you . . . well, you won't catch me stopping any bullets."

Dee took another step toward the door. "What do you want from me?"

"Nothing," said Abel. "At least nothing that you wouldn't want to do yourself."

"Like what?"

Lydia Abel smiled. Somehow the expression looked just as snooty as her usual sneer. "Like tell your dear friend Harley that she's about to die," she said.

Dee stopped moving. "What do you mean?" she asked. "Is that a threat?"

The dark-haired woman laughed again. "The world would be a much simpler place if I disposed of your friend, and it would give me considerable pleasure." She paused and stared off into space for a moment, as if considering the idea. "But no," she said at last. "Ms. Davisidaro is difficult, but she may yet prove a useful pawn in the great game."

"Harley's nobody's pawn," Dee protested loyally. Getting punched and kicked was bad enough, but listening to the woman talk about Harley was really starting to make Dee angry.

"In this game," replied Lydia Abel, "there are only

pawns." She kicked out suddenly and knocked over the music stand at her side. The metal stand clattered to the floor, and the book it had been holding fluttered down like a wounded bird. "But Cain is already gone. If Harley is going to fall, she should do it in some way that advances the cause he died for."

"What cause is that?"

The woman in the blue dress strolled gracefully among the metal chairs. "The greatest cause of all," she said. "Chaos."

Dee frowned, her progress toward the door momentarily forgotten. "Now I know you don't work for the same people as Cain. Cain didn't fight for chaos."

"Of course he did," Abel replied. A smile touched her lips again, and this time Dee thought it was actually sincere. "Cain was the greatest warrior of disorder. The true champion of unrest."

"No," Dee countered. "He only tried to keep the secret organizations from taking over."

"Precisely," replied Lydia Abel. She came closer to Dee, her dark blue eyes locked on Dee's round face as she walked. "The hidden chapters intend to impose order on the world—the order of their own rule. Only by preventing that order, by preserving chaos, can we stop them. We play them one against the other, grinding them all with storms of anarchy."

The idea had a certain twisted truth to it, but Dee still shook her head. "It doesn't have to be chaos."

Abel stopped in front of her. "You look on chaos as an evil thing," she said, "but you shouldn't. You've lived with chaos all your days. Order is a dead thing—chaos is life."

Dee was silent for a moment. Finally she nodded uncertainly. "Okay, cool. Chaos is life. Chaos is good. Chaos is cookie dough ice cream with extra cookies. Now, what has that got to do with anything?"

"More than you could ever understand," replied the woman, "but at the moment you need concern yourself only with warning your friend."

"I still don't know *why* I'm supposed to warn her," said Dee. "If you're not going to kill her, then why do I need to scare her?"

"Someone *else* is interested in your friend. *Very* interested. They're the ones she should be afraid of."

"Who are *they?*" asked Dee.

For the first time the confident expression on Abel's face slipped away. "I'm not sure," she admitted. "Whoever they are, they've done an impressive job of hiding their identity."

Dee looked into the woman's eyes and tried to get some sense of the truth of her statements, but Abel's eyes were as still and unreadable as mountain lakes. "Why don't you go to Harley yourself?"

Again the woman's expression revealed a trace of frustration and disappointment. "Because she's too well covered. If I go to her, they will see me. And if that happens, these people may kill us both."

"Hmmm," said Dee. "Why do I get the idea it's not Harley you're really worried about?"

Lydia Abel looked at her with a sneer that would

have insulted a cockroach. "Don't try to be funny, Ms. Janes. I'm not one of your little high-school pals. You don't have anything to say that would amuse me."

"Maybe not," said Dee. "But I have this." As fast as she could she hefted the metal music stand and hurled it toward the woman. Without waiting to see the impact, she turned and sprinted for the door.

Her fingers were on the doorknob when a hammer blow landed on the middle of her back. Okay, Dee thought. So maybe I *can't* beat her to the door. Then she fell breathless to the floor. A sensation of pins and needles flooded across her limbs, and her stomach roiled.

Lydia Abel grabbed her roughly by the left arm and flipped her over. "It seems you really are a slow learner," she said in a deathly quiet voice. "Perhaps if I broke a few bones, you would stop trying to be funny and take care of business. What do you think?"

Dee shook her aching head. "No thanks. I kind of like one-piece bones."

The woman sighed. "This may be hopeless, but let's try one more time," she said. "What I'm asking you to do is very simple. You like simple, don't you?"

"Sure," said Dee. The feeling was returning to her arms and legs, but she was definitely not in a mood to fight.

"That's good," said Abel. "Now, your very simple task is to go visit your friend Harley and tell her to get out of Stone Harbor as fast as possible. Do you understand?"

Dee nodded. "I understand," she answered. She carefully put her hands on the floor and pushed herself into a sitting position. "But you already said you wanted to hurt Harley. How do I know you aren't telling her to run just so you have an easier time picking her off?"

"You don't," said the woman. She leaned down and whispered into Dee's face. "Let me put it this way: You can go and warn your friend and maybe save her life, or you can decide you don't trust me, not warn her, and wait for the police to pick her up with a spoon and a plastic bag. What do you think?"

Dee rubbed her aching jaw. "Okay. I'll talk to her after school."

Abel nodded. "Good." She straightened and adjusted her blue dress. "Very good. You do that and maybe, *maybe* . . . I won't have to kill you."

NINE

The glass trembled in Harley's hand. She put down her drink and looked at the burger on her plate. She hadn't eaten breakfast and hadn't had dinner the night before, but she was still far too nervous to eat.

She glanced around the small diner. Agent Morris had promised to meet her at this address, but at the moment Harley saw only a handful of people sharing a booth near the wall and a single elderly woman sitting at the counter. None of them looked like agents from a government security agency—not that their appearance meant anything.

A waitress came around the counter and refilled Harley's soda. "You're not eating much, sweetie. Something wrong with that sandwich?"

Harley shook her head and smiled up at the woman. "No, it's fine. I guess I'm just not as hungry as I thought."

"Well, you should eat *something,*" the woman encouraged. "I know all you young girls want to be as thin as models, but you're too thin already. You should eat."

Harley picked up a french fry. "I'll try," she promised. She popped the hot slice of fried potato into her mouth and chewed. Apparently satisfied by this gesture, the waitress turned her attention to her other customers.

Over the next ten minutes Harley managed to eat

no more than a few bites of food. The idea of Noah and her father falling into the hands of Unit 17 had been enough to persuade Harley to participate in the NSA's experiment, but the thought of what she was about to do was still terrifying. She had seen Noah held in the grips of the sphere generator built by Unit 17. The energies generated within the device had been enormous, and the sphere itself had been unstable. Eventually the thing had taken a bite out of the Virginia countryside, almost swallowing Harley in the process.

Someone moved in the corner of the room. Harley looked up. For a moment she saw a woman in a white dress sitting in a booth no more than twenty feet away. Then, in a literal blink of her eyes, the woman was gone.

Harley shivered. Noah had visited her in dreams, but her visions of Noah had never leaked over into her conscious life. She wondered if the visits from her mother were actually the result of some kind of psychic phenomenon or if the constant stress of the past months had simply driven her crazy.

Out the diner window Harley saw a black sedan pull into the parking lot. A moment later another followed it. Then a third.

Harley tensed for a moment. The sedans looked exactly like those used by Unit 17. But Agent Morris stepped out of the first sedan and climbed the steps to the diner. With his dark suit and darker glasses Morris looked so much like a secret agent that he was almost a parody. Only his graying hair and the lines on his face betrayed the image. If Morris was a secret agent, he was an aging, tired one.

The NSA agent pulled off his glasses as he approached Harley's table. "You'll have to excuse us for being a little late, Ms. Davisidaro. We wanted to be sure that all security measures were in place. Are you ready to go?"

"Yes," Harley replied. She stood and licked her dry lips. She started to dig into her pocket for her small roll of cash, but Agent Morris pulled out a twenty and pitched it onto the table.

"Let me take care of it," he said. "If this works, your government is going to owe you a lot more than lunch."

Harley followed Agent Morris into the parking lot, where another NSA agent held open the back door of one of the sedans. Harley swallowed hard and got in.

The inside of the car was dark and quiet. Harley felt almost no sense of motion as the trio of cars left the parking lot and moved out onto the road. In a moment they were gliding smoothly along the highway to the north.

"How far are we going?" Harley asked.

"Not far," Agent Morris answered from the front seat. "Just sit back and relax. We should arrive in about ten minutes."

Harley leaned back into the padded seat and tried to gather her nerves. It was one thing to go up against Unit 17 soldiers or Umbra shadow men in a fight. Fights happened when you weren't expecting it, and there was just no time to be scared until they were over. But going off to face the sphere again left her nothing but time and fear. Only the thought that she might be able to rescue her father and Noah gave her the encouragement to keep from screaming.

I could see them today, she thought. It had been months since Noah had carried Harley's dying father into the white sphere. It had been so long that Harley had begun to wonder if she would ever see either of them again. Only her dream contact with Noah gave her hope. But if what Agent Morris said was true, a reunion might be no more than a few hours away.

The agent was right about one thing. No more than ten minutes after the little convoy left the diner outside of Stone Harbor, they turned off onto a narrow paved road. An automatic gate opened at their approach, and the sleek black cars eased into the parking lot of a small, modern office building.

"This is it?" Harley asked in surprise as she climbed out of the car.

"This is it," the agent replied. "Too plain for you?"

Harley shrugged. "It's just that the Unit 17 bases were so strange, and so huge. This place just looks too—"

"Normal?" Agent Morris nodded. "Come on inside, Ms. Davisidaro. I'll show you around."

The interior of the building looked almost as bland as the outside. There was a waiting room that would have suited a medical clinic and rows of small offices spaced along a hallway. Agent Morris led the way to a wooden door. "Here we are," he announced.

He pushed open the door to reveal a space approximately as large as the Stone Harbor High School gymnasium. Spaced around the room were a series of structures like gleaming metal telephone poles, and high above was a spiderweb of greenish wires. The floor was covered in a glossy, golden material, like a fabric of spun metal. The center of the room was dominated by a round platform of metal connected by a whole army of cables to both the floor and the overhead wires.

It was a complex, intimidating construction, but compared to the strange shapes and huge spaces of the machines Harley had seen at the Unit 17 bases, the NSA equipment seemed as ordinary as a VCR.

Harley stepped out onto the gleaming metal floor. Beneath the glossy surface the floor was soft and spongy. It sagged under Harley's weight as if she were walking on a huge marshmallow. "This place is so *small,*" she observed.

Agent Morris stepped up to her side and walked beside her across the soft floor. "We're proud of that," he said. "Unit 17's first efforts were crude devices, like building a transistor out of a lump of crystal. What you're seeing here is a second-generation facility. We've been able to reduce the size, cost, and power demand by a factor of twenty. Some of our scientists are predicting that we'll be able to make the whole thing small enough to fit in a suitcase."

Harley stopped in her steps. "You sound like you intend to build a lot more of these things."

"Only as many as are necessary to block action by others," the agent said. "We have to be ready to meet a threat in this arena, in the same way that nuclear weapons are the only possible deterrent against an enemy with their own nuclear weapons."

The analogy did little to settle Harley's nerves. The whole idea that she could be participating in the start of a new, and possibly even more dangerous, arms race was not exactly comforting. "Maybe this will be the end of it," she said hopefully. "Unit 17 has already lost two bases. They can't have an infinite amount of money. They can't afford to build new bases forever."

The NSA agent shrugged. "Their funds may not be endless, but the money they acquired from the government is substantial. It's hard to say at this point how much of that money was spent and how much still remains."

As they grew closer to the platform at the heart of the device, Harley saw that this was one part of the system that was actually larger than what she had seen before. The platform rim was well above the height of Harley's head, and the raised area spread out more than thirty feet across. As Harley and Morris neared the platform a woman in a white lab coat climbed down a ladder.

"Hello!" she called cheerfully. "Is this our new battery?"

"That's right," replied Agent Morris. He gestured toward Harley. "This is Kathleen Davisidaro."

The woman smiled. She appeared to be somewhere in her thirties, with blond hair that was pulled back in a ponytail and green eyes surrounded by nests of smile lines. She held her hand out to Harley. "Good morning, Kathleen. I'm Jean Lockwood. Welcome to the eye of the storm."

Harley didn't like the way Lockwood talked about her as if she were a piece of the machinery, but she took the woman's hand and shook it briefly. "What's 'the eye of the storm'?"

Agent Morris answered. "It's the code name this place was assigned," he explained. "Though I'm sure Dr. Lockwood will tell you there's been very little *calm* in this storm."

The blond woman laughed. "It *has* been a little busy around here." She released Harley's hand and gestured to the platform. "Well, Kathleen, are you ready to try it?"

Harley swallowed nervously. "Right now? Don't you have to get ready?"

"Don't worry," Dr. Lockwood replied. "We're not going to try to activate the equipment. This is just a test to see if you're going to be capable of powering the device."

"Oh." Even that was enough to make Harley nervous. After being treated and tortured by Umbra, Noah had demonstrated all sorts of paranormal abilities, and since he had gone into the sphere, his powers had increased even more. But Harley wasn't sure that her own abilities amounted to much. She was afraid to learn that she had agreed to the experiment only to find that she didn't have the power needed to create the sphere. That meant she wouldn't be seeing her father or Noah anytime soon.

Dr. Lockwood led the way around the platform to a padded chair resting amidst a cluster of dials, monitors, and keyboards. "Have a seat over here, and we'll get started."

Harley eased herself into the chair. "What do I do?" she asked. "I don't have any idea where to begin."

"You can begin by rolling up your sleeve," said Dr. Lockwood.

"What?"

The woman reached over to a tray and picked up a syringe filled with clear fluid. "I'm going to give you a little shot," she said. "Nothing big, just a small tranquilizer."

Harley looked at the needle and frowned. "Do I have to?"

Dr. Lockwood shook her head. "No, we can carry on without this if you want. But our tests have shown that nervousness can significantly decrease the output of the transalpha waves necessary for this experiment. Do you think you can remain calm during the attempt?"

Harley thought for a moment. As much as she hated the idea of getting a shot, she didn't want to do anything that would prevent her from generating the sphere. "No," she said. "I guess you better go ahead and jab me."

"Don't worry," Dr. Lockwood said in a soothing voice. She picked up a cotton swab and spread icy alcohol over the inside of Harley's arm. "This won't hurt."

"That's what they always say."

Dr. Lockwood nodded. "And it never does hurt . . . me." She plunged the syringe smoothly into the muscle of Harley's arm and slowly depressed the plunger. When the device was empty, she pulled the needle free. "There," she said. "How did that feel?"

"It hurt," Harley replied.

"Funny," said Dr. Lockwood. "I didn't feel a thing. Hang on a few seconds—we should get a response to the injection very quickly. Do you feel anything?"

Harley shook her head. "No, I . . ." She heard a noise. It started high overhead and fell like the whistle of an approaching bomb. The noise rose in a sudden explosion of sound, and when it did, the world shattered like a mirror struck by a hammer.

Harley flew. She soared through featureless infinite space toward a pinprick of light as faint as a birthday candle seen across a lake. Harley drifted toward the light. Her pace grew faster. Other lights swept by to her left and right, smeared into streaks by her ever increasing speed. The light became brighter. Brighter. Blinding. Harley closed her eyes, but it did no good. The light was everywhere, inside her as well as out. It was searing. Painful. All consuming.

Harley screamed.

When she opened her eyes, she was sitting in a field of dry brown grass. Thin streams of clouds drifted across a tired blue sky, and tiny puffs of thistledown drifted among the grass. A flight of quail broke from the grass as Harley rose slowly to her feet. The brown birds traveled no more than fifty yards before dropping back into the stalks.

Nearby something was moving through the grass.

Harley shook off her disorientation and hurried toward the sound. "Mom?" she called. "Mom, is that you?"

She burst from the edge of the tall grass and found herself at the edge of a wood. Slipping between the trees was a slender figure in a white dress.

"Mom!" Harley ran into the woods after the departing figure. Even under the trees, the world was dry and dead. Leaves puffed to dust at Harley's touch, and vines crumbled from the tree trunks as she slipped past. She circled the trunk of a huge birch and found the woman in white less than a hundred yards ahead. Harley put on a burst of speed.

A gut-wrenching moment of disorientation seized Harley, and the forest disappeared like a television set that had been switched off. She found herself in a place lit by harsh lights and stark shadows. A metallic taste coated her mouth, pain seared her head, and a heavy feeling settled over her body. She tried to move, but she could get no sense of her arms and legs. Her body seemed wooden. Dead.

A blurry shadow fell over her. "We're getting a peak in the forty-kilowatt range," murmured a distorted, dragging voice. "But she can't sustain the output."

Harley blinked in an effort to clear her vision. Even blinking was an exhausting effort.

The shadow above her shifted. Its shape twisted, pulsed, and flowed like a person walking in front of a line of fun-house mirrors. Harley thought she could recognize the outline of Dr. Lockwood's face in the cloudy, mangled forms, but she couldn't be sure.

"She's coming out of it," said the slow voice. "Performance has dropped by thirty percent."

Another voice spoke in a deep and distorted rumble. Harley couldn't make out a word of what the second voice said.

A hand reached down from the twisted mass above her. She felt fingers pressed into the soft skin of her throat.

"Applying booster," said the voice.

A moment of sharp pain, and then . . .

Harley staggered and almost fell. She regained her balance in time to be tripped by a root and only saved herself from hitting the ground by grabibng onto the rough trunk of an ancient maple.

She was in the forest. This time there was no sign of the field and its high grass. Instead heavy trunks of sycamore, birch, oak, and hickory surrounded Harley in all directions. The massive trees soared into the air like the pillars holding up the roof of some vast cathedral. From that invisible roof a slow, steady shower of multicolored leaves fell. The constant rain of foliage settled to the earth with a faint hiss, like static from a broken radio. The leaves blanketed the ground in a carpet of brown, gold, and orange that was unbroken, knee-deep, and as dry as old bones. Here and there the canopy had thinned to the point where sunlight could reach the ground in irregular patches. But these spots of light only made the rest of the forest seem all the more gloomy.

Between the thick, dark trunks of the trees Harley

saw a patch of white moving among the shadows. She pushed herself away from the maple tree and ran toward the vanishing point of brightness.

The sound of leaves smashing under Harley's feet seemed as loud as a freight train. The leaves were terribly, impossibly dry. They didn't just crunch—they exploded, turning into puffs of brown dust as she crushed them. She left a thick brown cloud of leaf dust in her wake.

The woman in white was walking away from Harley, but she was walking slowly. Harley cut the distance between them to fifty yards, then thirty, then . . .

Light flared across Harley's vision, quickly replaced by darkness. Then light. She was lying on a cold metal table, being wheeled down a hallway. This time her vision was better. She could see Dr. Lockwood hurrying beside the table on her right, with Agent Morris on the left.

"What if we increase the booster?" suggested Agent Morris in a breathless voice. "Would that provide the needed duration?"

"I doubt it," Lockwood replied. "We might get more output at the peak, but the duration would probably decrease, not increase."

Harley licked her dry lips and tried to speak. Her tongue felt swollen to the size of a subway car. Her teeth were a line of jagged mountains. She got her mouth open and managed a wordless groan.

Dr. Lockwood looked down at her. "Lie still," she ordered. "This won't take long."

"Wha . . . ," groaned Harley. "Wha . . . happen . . ."

131

"Just a small problem with the test," the doctor answered. "Don't worry. We'll have it all taken care of in a few minutes."

To Harley it felt like more than a small problem. If the *test* was this bad, she couldn't imagine what it would be like when it came time to actually power the sphere.

The foot of the table smashed open a pair of double doors, and Harley found herself in a room lit by harsh greenish yellow lights. A stack of equipment loomed at the far end of the room, and a series of consoles seemed to grow like fungus from the walls. From her angle Harley had a hard time telling what any of the equipment was designed to do, but it all had a very familiar—and disquieting—appearance.

Agent Morris shifted around the end of the bed and peered down at her. "You're certain this is necessary?" he asked.

Dr. Lockwood stepped over to his side and nodded. "Full encapsulation is the only way to get continuous output over a long period of time. We saw that with the previous subject."

Full encapsulation. Harley wasn't sure what the words meant, but they certainly didn't sound good. "Wai . . . ," she slurred. "Don . . ."

Then she was in the forest again, running fast through a grove of boxwood. The rapid transition left her dizzy, but she was thrilled to see that the woman in white was just a dozen paces ahead. Harley sprinted forward and reached out her hand to touch the woman.

And she was back on the table. The mass of equipment

was closer this time. It seemed to be one complex, central machine, with a huge plastic cylinder at its core. Furls, knobs, and shelves protruded from the rest of the device in a way that made the whole thing seem half formed and alien. She knew she had seen a device like it before, but her shaken mind couldn't quite determine when.

From beside the table Harley heard Dr. Lockwood heave a heavy sigh. "She's so much like her mother."

"Mother," repeated Harley.

She was in the forest. The woman in white was an arm's length away. Sudden fear jumped in Harley, but it was too late to stop. She reached out and touched the woman on the arm.

The figure in white turned slowly. Long before it had finished its pirouette, Harley's breath froze in her chest. Her fear turned into a blind, mindless panic.

The woman had no face. A yellowed, dry skull gaped at her. Empty eye sockets. A dark gash of a nose. The exposed jaw sagged open in a terrible, lipless grin.

Harley screamed. She opened her mouth wide and screamed until her throat burned.

It wasn't even the pure awfulness of the skull that made her scream. She screamed because in the space of a second, she saw an image of a room in the dry sockets of the skull's empty eyes. It was a room filled with devices and equipment and a . . .

. . . clear tube. Harley was inside a tube.

Through the curved surface she saw Lockwood and Morris moving around in the room. Their faces and bodies stretched and shrank as their images refracted across the curved surface of the cylinder surrounding Harley.

Whatever Dr. Lockwood had injected into Harley was still making her limbs feel sluggish and heavy, but she managed to raise her hand and push weakly against the smooth surface of the tube.

Agent Morris noticed her motion and stepped closer to the cylinder. "I see you're awake," he said. His words were muffled to a faint whisper by the cube. "Unfortunately you won't be awake for long."

Harley struggled to overcome her fear and the lingering numbness in her mouth. "Let . . . me . . . out," she said, pronouncing each word carefully.

The NSA agent only shook his head. "Sorry," he replied. "Can't do that."

"Why?" asked Harley. "Why . . . are . . . you . . . doing . . . this?"

Agent Morris smiled. "Remember when I said that Unit 17 had found someone to power their device?" he asked. His face broke into a wide grin. "Well, you're the someone."

He signaled to Dr. Lockwood, and the blond woman's fingers danced across the strange controls of the device surrounding the tube. A hissing, chugging sound echoed through the tube. Yellow fluid began to pour rapidly into the cylinder.

"No," gasped Harley. Her first cry was weak, but as adrenaline flushed the last of the drugs from her body her shouts rapidly gained strength. "No! Let me out! Let me out, you—"

Her pleading was cut off as the yellow fluid covered her mouth.

TEN

A ghost was in the house.

Scott stared at the bank of black-and-white video monitors and rubbed his tired eyes. Four times in the last hour something had tripped the security system within the mansion, but so far he hadn't seen anything. The false alarms were probably caused by a glitch in the central processor or an oversensitive sensor reacting to air currents. Whatever it was, it was majorly irritating.

For the tenth time in as many minutes Scott checked his watch. It was after one. He had hoped for Rhinehardt's return for more than an hour, but he hadn't really expected it. Despite what the Legion agent said as he was leaving, Scott didn't believe he himself had anything to do with the secret organization and its generations-long experiment. And he didn't think Chloe was one of their little clones, either. Now that Rhinehardt had gone, Scott doubted Chloe had ever had anything to do with Legion at all.

The whole story had been nothing more than an excuse to come into Kenyon's mansion and raid every scrap of information they'd been collecting for over a year. There was far more information contained in the computers than just Scott's search for Chloe. The databases held everything Scott, Kenyon, and Harley had learned about Legion, Umbra, Unit 17, and the unnamed fourth agency that had employed Agent Cain. Now that the house was empty and Scott had time to think about it, he was positive that the whole thing had been a complete scam—a disguised data raid on their systems. And he had fallen for it hook, line, and sinker.

He couldn't remember a time when he had felt so stupid in his whole life. The Legion agent could have told him *anything* as long as it offered a chance of finding Chloe, and Scott would have believed every lie. He had become so blind to everything but the idea of finding Chloe that he had even managed to push away Dee, the one person who had really cared for him in five years. If it had been possible to kick himself hard in the butt, Scott would have done it.

Scott wondered if he should just sneak out of town before Kenyon got back from Chicago. A note of apology to both Kenyon and Dee, and he could be out of here. Running away would be a lot easier than confessing what he had done. And everyone would probably be happier to see him gone.

The alarm panel beeped again and a code appeared announcing that a motion sensor had been tripped. Scott frowned at the machine and tapped out a quick command on the security console. The scene on the monitors changed to four angled shots of the lower hallway. Scott examined the screens closely, then shook his head. "Worthless," he muttered. Kenyon's obsession with security had filled the house with so many gizmos that one of them always seemed to be going off. Scott felt a fresh sense of guilt as he realized all Kenyon's efforts had been for nothing—Scott had let the enemy into the house through the front door.

Another motion sensor beeped. This time Scott was angry enough to slam his hand down on the system. "Oh, shut *up*," he muttered to the machine. He reached for the switch that would turn the whole system off. But before he could throw it, he saw the ghost.

Scott brought his face up close to one of the security screens and stared at the image. Something *was* there, but it was hard to say exactly what that something was. It didn't seem to be a person, an animal, or even a floating sphere. There was only a rippling wave of distortion that slowly crossed the screen. Scott panned the camera to follow the moving disturbance. The ripples moved down the hallway past a bookshelf, then disappeared.

For several minutes Scott stared at the screen. His eyes began to water from the effort of trying to spot the ghost again, but the shape was gone. He leaned back in his chair and tried to think of what he should do.

Something was in the house. At first the idea of this transparent invader didn't scare Scott as badly as it might have. After seeing Rhinehardt call the red sphere, he knew that Legion was capable of some tricks that he didn't understand. And Legion certainly knew the location of the house. Scott figured that this new apparition had to be connected with Rhinehardt's visit. And if the agent had sent this thing to the house, it might mean that he was coming back soon. The appearance of the strange ghostly form could be a good sign.

Unless it's something he sent to get you out of the way,

a frightened voice suggested in the back of Scott's mind.

Most of the time Scott wasn't very good at being paranoid. He concentrated on making the technology work and let Kenyon focus on the worrying. But as Scott's mind began to race he quickly traced through a trail of logic that led to fear.

He had been worried about Rhinehardt getting away with their information. Surely Rhinehardt would be worried about the Legion information that Scott had learned. After all, Legion was a secret organization, and their technology of brain-computers and high-tech breeding programs was completely unknown to the world. Legion had to be concerned that Scott might find some way to use what he had seen. They must have some measures for silencing those people who had gotten a peek at their advanced technology.

Another of the motion sensors tripped, this time in the downstairs library. Scott scrambled to turn on the cameras in that room. Once again he saw a space of disturbance moving through the room.

Rhinehardt hadn't returned, but it seemed obvious that he had sent something to the mansion—something searching the house room by room.

Scott looked around the security station and the adjacent computer room. There seemed to be nothing that could serve as a weapon, but Scott did spot one device he could use. He crossed quickly to a workstation and picked up a small metal box with a flat LCD panel set into one side. He hefted the instrument and twisted the central dial.

The device was the latest version of Scott's paranormal energy detector. The invention had proved capable of detecting an unusual electromagnetic radiation put out by people like Harley who had some special, undeniable gift. If the thing in the house contained some of the same kind of information, Scott would at least have a way to see the invader's progress.

The instant he turned it on, the screen went to a solid, unbroken white, and the numeric display at the bottom of the display flashed a wild stream of values. For a moment he thought the detector was broken.

Scott cranked down the strength of the detector to one-half normal, then to a tenth, and finally to the minimum position—a hundred times less sensitive than normal. Finally the brilliant white field shrank to a point on the screen and the numbers became more reasonable. The thing on the lower floor was definitely producing psychic energy. In fact, it was producing that energy at a rate greater than anything Scott had measured.

And it was moving his way.

Scott glanced frantically around the room. He had his detector, but he still didn't know what he was facing, and he had no idea how to fight it. He ran out of the room and opened Kenyon's gun closet. There were plenty of guns to choose from, but none of them seemed quite right for shooting at some invisible energy beast. Somehow Scott doubted that the red sphere that had burned through the kitchen window would have been slowed by a bullet, either. The sphere seemed to be no more solid than a breath of wind, yet it certainly contained enough energy to kill. If the thing downstairs had no body to shoot at, then even an elephant gun might not stop it.

Instead Scott lifted a heavy-duty Taser from the bottom of the closet. The Taser was usually used to stun an opponent, not to kill, but at full power the sleek black unit could deliver over half a million volts of electricity. That was enough to drop a charging bull in its tracks or to stop a human's heart. Scott only hoped it was enough to stop a ghost.

With the detector in one hand and the Taser in the other, Scott returned to the security console. No more motion sensors or other devices had been tripped, but if the thing had come in from outside, it had certainly passed by dozens of sensors without being noticed. The security system wasn't reliable when it came to this creature.

Scott consulted his energy detector. According to the screen, the ghost was on its way up the stairs. Scott gave a moment's consideration to meeting the thing in the central hall. That would give him a clear shot with the Taser. But the hall was too open, too spacious for a fight. He dragged a worktable across the computer room and crouched behind it. If the ghost was going to come to him, it would have to come through the door of the computer room. And when it did, Scott would deliver five hundred thousand volts of discouragement.

He watched as the glowing spot on the detector screen reached the top of the stairs. The security system remained stubbornly silent as the energy source crossed the central hall, bypassed the bedrooms, and walked straight toward the point where Scott was hiding.

His grip on the Taser grew slippery as his hands began to sweat. He trembled and fought to keep his breathing steady as the ghost grew closer.

The numbers at the bottom of the screen grew smaller. The point of energy was in the hallway, no more than thirty meters away. Twenty-five. Twenty.

Scott carefully put down the detector and steadied the Taser with both hands. Sweat rolled down his forehead and dripped into his eyes. He glanced down at the detector.

The ghost had stopped just outside the door.

For what seemed like an hour but was probably no more than twenty seconds, Scott held his aim on the open door. Finally he cleared his throat. "I'm armed!" he shouted. "If you come in here, I'll shoot!"

A moment of silence followed, broken by a voice speaking from the hallway. "Would you really shoot me, Scott?"

A girl stepped into the room.

Scott's eyes went wide. The Taser dropped from his hands and clattered on the tile floor.

Five years had turned the short curls imposed by the Benevolence Home into waves of honey blond hair that spilled around the girl's shoulders like curtains of buttermilk silk. Five years had added curves to a straight figure and turned an adventurous young tomboy into the most stunning woman Scott had ever seen. But five years wasn't enough for him to forget a single feature of her face or the glint of mischief in her extraordinary eyes.

"Chloe," he breathed in a choked whisper. He stood up from behind the table and started across the computer room. His knees trembled, and every muscle in his body seemed to be made from loose rubber bands. He stumbled toward her like an infant learning its first steps.

Chloe Adair rushed to him and threw her arms around him. "Oh, Scott. It really is you!"

Scott opened his mouth to speak. He had rehearsed a hundred lines over the years for just this event. He had thought of being witty, or funny, or serious. But when the moment came, he could only gasp for air. He put his long arms around Chloe, pulled her tight against him, and gave in to his tears.

It was minutes before Scott got control of himself, but Chloe didn't try to push him away. She held on to him just as tightly as he held her. Finally Scott stepped back and looked down into her face. "How . . . how did you get here?" he asked. "How did you find me?"

There were tears on Chloe's face as well. They made twin silvery streaks along the curve of her high cheekbones and glimmered like jewels in her long lashes. "I heard you," she said. "You were looking for me, and I heard you." She smiled. It was the same quirky, off-center, completely dazzling smile that Scott remembered. "At first I didn't know it was you. Even when the computers said it was, I didn't really believe it. I thought the machines had to be wrong." She paused and drew in a deep breath.

"You don't know how glad I am that *I'm* the one who was wrong!" She buried her face against his chest again, and her back shivered with sobs.

Scott held her again and rocked her gently back and forth. He closed his eyes and felt a warm flow of some perfect, unnameable emotion flooding through his body like lava from a mystical volcano. For five years he had lived every day with a burden pressing on his heart. Even when he wasn't thinking about Chloe, her absence was with him. The dark tunnel and the terror of that day beneath the orphanage had never left him.

The lifting of the burden left him feeling elated, but also a little off balance. Chloe is found. She was lost, but she's here. With me. She's solid, and alive, and well, and we're together again. Scott wondered how long it would be before the truth of those words really made it into his brain.

"I've been looking for you for—" He stopped and swallowed a lump in his throat. "For a long time. Were you looking for me?"

Chloe dropped her arms and stepped back. Her full lips pressed together. "No," she admitted. She lowered her face. "I never looked because . . . because I thought you were dead. I thought you died that night in the tunnel." Her back heaved again as she fought off another sob. "I thought I was alone."

"What happened to you?" Scott asked. "Where have you been all this time?"

Chloe raised her gaze to Scott's face and smiled again. "That doesn't matter now," she said. "I'll tell you all about it later. All that matters is that we're together."

Scott couldn't help smiling back. "You're right. That's all that counts."

Chloe reached out and took both his hands in hers. "Come on," she said. "We better get ready to go."

"Go?" Scott frowned. "Go where?"

"We have to leave this place," said Chloe. "And we have to go *soon.*" She gave his hands a squeeze. "I came here to save your life."

ELEVEN

Dee Janes was living proof of the origin of stress. There was something she *had* to do, but someone was standing in her way. "Harley needs my help," she repeated for what seemed like the hundredth time.

Her mother looked at her across the dinner table and shook her head. "You're not leaving this house, young lady," she said primly.

Dee swallowed her anger and tried to be calm. Her parents were bright, intelligent people with her best interest at heart. They couldn't help it if they were idiots. She turned and tried her appeal on her father. "You said you cared about Harley. If I don't go out and talk to her, she might be killed."

Her father shook his head. "Somehow you're missing a very basic concept here, Dee. When the word *killed* appears in a sentence, I don't want you to have anything to do with it. Understand?"

"But Harley—"

"I've already sent a car to check on the beach house," her father replied. "If there's anything suspicious going on, we'll know about it soon enough."

Dee wished that it wasn't out of fashion for a seventeen-year-old to throw a fit. She felt like a little stomping the floor and screaming was exactly what she needed. Instead she tried to be reasonable.

145

"That's not good enough," she said. "Harley wasn't at school today. I've been calling all afternoon, and there's no answer. And it's not just Harley—there's no answer at Scott and Kenyon's place. They could both be in big trouble."

"It'll have to be good enough," her father replied. "If Officer Travis finds anything wrong—"

"You sent Travis?" Dee asked in exasperation.

Her father's eyebrows lowered over his gray eyes. "And what's wrong with Officer Travis?"

Dee snorted. "Nothing, as long as you don't mind that he's *stupid.*"

It was the wrong thing to say. Her father had been the police chief in town for more than a decade, and he took a lot of pride in his men. "Kirk Travis is a fine officer," he said in a cold voice. "I'm sure he'll let us know if there's anything wrong."

Dee's mother joined the attack. "I know that you're concerned about your friend," she said. "Your father and I are fond of Harley, too. But we're more concerned about you."

The phone rang. Dee jumped up to answer it, but her father waved her back to her seat. "Hang on," he said. "It's probably just Travis calling to say that everything is fine." He got up and walked into the living room to answer the phone.

Dee's mother reached out and touched her daughter on the arm. "It's going to be fine, honey," she said. "Just wait and see."

"Sure," Dee replied. She wanted to ask her mother if she considered shadow men who could freeze with a

146

touch, floating balls of red fire, and guns that fired blasts of lightning to be part of her definition of "fine," but admitting that she had seen these things herself didn't seem like a very good idea.

A second later Dee's father walked back into the room. "It's your office," he said to his wife. "Some people are out there right now who would like to take a look at the Richardson place."

Dee's mother was up like a shot. "I've been trying to unload that house for a year," she said. She cast a quick glance at Dee. "You think you can handle Dee if I go over to show the house?"

"Don't worry," Dee's father answered with a nod. "I'll take care of our little renegade. You go right ahead."

It didn't take any more encouragement to send Dee's mother running for the door. "If I sell this one," she called, "we're moving to a bigger house ourselves!" She went through the door, and a moment later Dee heard her car speed away from the house.

Alone with her father, Dee turned her attention back to the subject of the evening. "Look, you've seen these guys from Unit 17. Do you really think Kirk the Jerk can handle them?"

Her father's face was as hard as stone. "Officer Travis will call us if there's any problem," he said. "And even if he does, you're not going out there, so you can just forget it." Dee opened her mouth to reply, but her father cut her off with a raised finger. "I believe we've had enough of this conversation for now. Don't you have some homework?"

Dee nodded slowly. "Yes, sir. I believe I do."

She pushed her chair away from the table and walked up the stairs with a liberal dose of teenage sullenness applied to each step. Once she was in her room, she slammed the door and went immediately to the phone. There was no answer at Harley's and no answer at Kenyon and Scott's place, but Dee had been expecting that. The next number she dialed was the Stone Harbor Police Department.

In a town the size of Stone Harbor no more than five officers were on the job at any time. On an average Thursday night that number was no more than three.

The phone was answered on the first ring. "Police department," said the voice of a police dispatcher who Dee had known all her life. "Is there is an emergency?"

Dee cleared her throat and did her best to lower her voice. "You're not *kidding* it's an emergency!" she cried. "This is Louise, um . . . Louise Losageles down at the South County Grill."

"Louise *who?*"

Dee ignored the question. "You better hurry!" she barked into the phone. "We've got a big fight going on in our parking lot!"

"Yes, ma'am," replied the dispatcher. "We'll send a car right away."

"No!" Dee shouted. "A car won't do it. This isn't just a fight. It's . . . it's more like a *riot*. One car isn't going to do it. You better send every officer in town. Send the fire department, too!" She hung up the phone quickly before the dispatcher could ask any questions.

While she waited for a response, Dee went to the closet and pulled out a dark blue windbreaker. It was still cool at night, and she wanted the darkest clothing she could find. Then she kicked off her shoes and started lacing on a pair of black sneakers. She was still tying the shoes when the phone rang again.

Two rings later her father answered. Thirty seconds after that she heard him slam down the phone. "Dee!" he called up the stairs.

"Yes," she called back.

"I have to run out for a few minutes. You're not to leave the house, right?"

Dee considered arguing. Giving in too easily might be a tip-off. But she wanted her father out of the house before anyone had a chance to swing by the South County Grill and see that the place was, in fact, just fine. "Sure," she replied. "I don't like it, but I'll be good."

"I'll be back in ten minutes," her father shouted. "Twenty at the most."

Dee waited until she heard his car start and saw the lights shining down the driveway. Then she headed downstairs on the run.

Like almost every police officer in the country, Dee's father carried a semiautomatic pistol. But before he had changed to the new gun a few years ago, he had packed away the policeman's traditional companion: a .38-caliber revolver. The old pistol was stowed in a metal box at the top of the closet, and there was a trigger lock on the gun. It took Dee less than a minute to retrieve the keys to both the lock and the box from their "secret" hiding place, extract the gun and a half-empty box of bullets, and slide the whole arrangement into the pocket of her wind-breaker. Then she hurried into the kitchen to collect her purse.

Until that point Dee's hastily constructed plan had functioned like clockwork. But all plans fall apart somewhere.

Her purse was sitting in the middle of the kitchen table, and it was wide open. As soon as Dee looked at it her heart sank. And when she glanced inside, her worst fears were confirmed—her father had taken her car keys.

She spent the next minute letting out every colorful phrase she had ever picked up from the prisoners in the city's small jail. Then she went to the window. Stone Harbor had no cab service. Dee could think of several friends who might be willing to give her a lift, but she could think of none that she wanted to get involved in this situation. Her parents were right about that much—what was going on with Harley was *dangerous*.

She went over the distances in her head. Three miles out to Harley's beach house. Maybe four. From there she figured it was another four or five miles to the mansion. Nine miles, tops. Two summers before, Dee had hiked nineteen miles in one day at Camp Greenleaf, and that had been in the woods. Nine miles on the road would be a piece of cake.

She went to the refrigerator door and wrote a quick note on the erasable display board.

Sorry, but I had to go. Love you, D.

Then she slipped out the door and started running down the street.

Dee managed to run for a little over three blocks, then she slowed to a walk. The sun had gone down half an hour before, but the sky in the west was still blue. She figured she had at least another hour before it would really be dark.

A car approached. Dee hurried off the road and waited nervously until it passed. The South County Grill was almost ten miles south of downtown, and it would take a few minutes for the officers to gather and determine that it had all been a hoax. But once the trick was revealed, Dee expected it would take her father about ten milliseconds to figure out who was behind the fake call. She didn't want to be caught before she even had a chance to check on Harley and Scott.

The car passed, and Dee jogged on. For the next thirty minutes she alternated between a walk and a run. She took advantage of the long downhill stretch leading to the coast road to lengthen out her stride. For a few hundred yards she imagined she was running almost as fast as Harley did. But once she was on the level ground at the bottom of the hill, Dee quickly regretted her burst of speed. Sharp cramps in both legs forced her to a snail's pace for the next half mile.

It was dark by the time she reached the city limits. Hiding every time she heard a car approach was definitely slowing her down, but if she didn't stay away from the road, her father was sure to have her back home in ten minutes—if he resisted the impulse to hurl her into a jail cell.

She tried walking along the beach, but the sand wore her out faster than the gravel along the road, so she went back to her routine of ducking and hiding. Eight o'clock came and went, and nine. By the time Harley's beach house appeared on a curving stretch of pale sand, Dee was beginning to think that the counselors back at Lake Greenleaf had been telling one big whopper of a fib. There was no way she could have ever hiked nineteen miles without having a coronary.

Approaching the beach house gave Dee a temporary boost of excitement. There were no lights on and no police cars in sight as she jogged the last hundred yards to the house. There were also no open doors.

Dee cupped her hands around her face and peered through the sliding glass doors on the sea side of the house. No furniture was overturned, and nothing seemed to be messed up. If there had been a fight in the house, it wasn't obvious. She pulled back her hand and hammered on the glass. "Harley! Harley, are you in there?"

She received no answer. Dee contemplated smashing the window with a rock, but she didn't see much point in the action. If Harley was gone, she was gone. If someone had taken her away by force, Dee doubted that those people had left a business card.

She turned with a sigh and looked around the curve of the harbor toward Kenyon's mansion. The big house was out of sight behind bluffs and trees, and it was farther away from Harley's house than Harley's house was from town. But it was also the only other place Dee could think to go. She started up the gravel drive back to the highway.

Maybe I can get somebody I *don't* like to give me a lift, she thought. That way if they get killed, it's no big loss. She stopped to massage a charley horse out of her thigh. Maybe I should call a cheerleader.

She was almost back to the highway when a vehicle turned out of the traffic and headed toward her along the narrow drive. Dee looked left and right, but there was nothing to hide behind, just flat expanses of tan sand and thin growths of saw grass. She staggered to a stop. As long as her father was going to catch her, anyway, there was no point in running further.

But as the vehicle drew near, Dee saw that it wasn't a police car. In fact, it wasn't even a car. A single headlight pinned Dee in the center of the drive as the roar of a motorcycle engine grew closer.

The rider skidded to a stop twenty feet away. He wore a black leather jacket and a black helmet and a dark face shield that covered his features. The bike was also jet black, with gleaming chrome pipes.

Great, thought Dee. Harley gets kidnapped by some secret group, I'm running from the police, and then I get picked up by Renegade Biker Dude. "Hi," she said. "Um, this is private property."

The motorcycle rider reached down and killed the engine. "I know," he said, his voice muffled by the face shield. Then he reached up and pulled off the black helmet to reveal the face of Kenyon Moor. "It's *my* property," he said.

Dee stared at him in astonishment. "What are you doing on that thing?"

"This *thing* is a Harley-Davidson Sportster 880, the same model that Harley lost," said Kenyon. "I thought I'd surprise her with a little present."

"A little present." Dee shook her head. For a guy with a billion bucks in the bank, Kenyon didn't have a clue when it came to dating. "If you're buying motorcycles, then the big money talks must have gone well."

He nodded. "Well enough. I called ahead to Boston and purchased the bike, then drove it down here." He craned his neck and tried to see past Dee. "Do you think Harley will like the present?"

"I think Harley will *love* the bike," said Dee. "Only Harley's not here."

Kenyon frowned. "Where is she?"

Dee shrugged. "Oh, I think she's been kidnapped by another secret group."

Kenyon's eyes widened in shock. "You're kidding."

"'Fraid not." Dee walked around to the side of the bike. "Have you been out to the mansion?"

"No." Kenyon shook his head. "I came straight here."

"Then you better scoot forward and let me on," said Dee.

"Why?"

"Because I think Scott's gone, too." She pushed Kenyon forward and climbed onto the back of the motorcycle. Together they roared back onto the highway and sped north.

TWELVE

Chloe sipped from a cup of tea and glanced nervously out the window. "We really should be going," she said.

Scott bit his lip. "Are you sure?"

"It's very important," said Chloe. "You've already seen how badly Legion wants me back. And they certainly will try to eliminate you. You know too much. They know where you are, and they could be back here at any moment. If Legion gets their hands on us, they'll kill you and lock me up forever."

"We'll go as soon as Kenyon comes," said Scott. "He should be here any minute."

A look of concern crossed Chloe's face. "Scott, that's what you've been saying for the last two hours." She put down her cup, reached out, and touched him gently on the back of his hand. "I don't want to leave without you, Scott. Please, say you'll come with me."

Now that he had found her again, the idea of being away from Chloe was the most frightening thing Scott could think of. "I'll come," he agreed. "Just let me talk to Kenyon."

Chloe nodded, but from the expression on her face she obviously wasn't happy about the idea. "You'll have to convince your friend Kenyon to leave this place, too," she said. "He's known to Legion and Unit 17. They're sure to come for him."

155

"I'll warn him," said Scott. "But I don't know if he'll go. Kenyon's more likely to buy a tank and wait for them to come."

"I see." Chloe picked up her cup and sipped again at her tea. "Well, I wish him luck." She gestured at the kitchen window with its melted glass. "He's going to need it."

Scott glanced at the clock on the wall. He had been expecting Kenyon for hours. Kenyon had called from Chicago to say that he didn't need a ride from the airport, but that had been many hours before. Scott was beginning to wonder if something had happened to Kenyon on his way back to Stone Harbor.

"We should call Harley and Dee," Scott suggested. "They need to know where we're going."

Chloe raised a fine eyebrow. "Who are they?"

"They're friends." Scott gave a brief explanation of Harley's story and how she had lost both her father and Noah to Unit 17.

"I haven't heard of her," said Chloe. "I don't think she's in any of the secret databases, so she's probably safe where she is."

Scott was relieved to hear that much. Harley had been through so much, she deserved a little peace and quiet for a while. "What about Dee?"

Chloe shook her head. "Who is she?"

"Dee's my girl . . ." Scott stopped in the middle of the word and started again. "Dee's a friend. She helped me get Kenyon and Harley away from Unit 17, and she helped me search for you."

"Oh." Chloe looked at Scott over the rim of her cup. "And you really like this girl Dee."

Scott nodded. "Yeah, I guess I do."

Chloe smiled. "That's good," she said. "I'm glad you had someone to help you get through the lonely times."

Scott felt confused and a little embarrassed. He was thrilled to have Chloe back, but talking to her about Dee seemed like a . . . betrayal. The only thing was, Scott wasn't sure who it was he was supposed to have betrayed. He had always told Dee that Chloe was like his sister. In a sense that was true. They had grown up together, and there was no one he had ever felt closer to. She was his only family. But of course, Chloe wasn't really his sister. Now that she was back, now that he had seen her, he found that his feelings for Chloe were no longer so clear.

"What about you?" Scott asked, hoping to change the direction of the conversation. "You must have made some friends in the last five years."

"Some." Chloe smiled. "You'll get to meet them when you come with me."

"We're going to your home?"

"Absolutely," Chloe said with a nod. "I have a very safe, isolated place. It's probably the best place we could possibly go to hide from Legion."

"But what about Umbra?" Scott asked.

"Umbra?"

Scott nodded. "That night in the tunnel back at Old Benny. Those people in the robes belonged to a group called Umbra."

"I know," Chloe replied.

"Well, how did you get away from them?" Scott asked. He smiled and leaned toward her. "That must have been some adventure."

But Chloe didn't seem excited about telling the story. She sat her cup down on the edge of the table and looked at Scott for a long moment before speaking. "Scott, I never got away from Umbra."

"What?"

"I'm still in Umbra," said Chloe. "I didn't get away from them—I joined them."

Scott felt his stomach do a flip-flop. He pulled back from Chloe in surprise and horror. "But Chloe . . ."

She reached out quickly and took hold of his hand. "It's not like you think, Scott. All you've seen of Umbra is what Wilhelmina made of the eastern order."

"Wilhelmina?"

"The woman—the *thing*—that called itself Billie." Chloe closed her eyes for a moment and shivered. "She took the eastern chapters of Umbra and perverted them into something horrible. The rest of the organization is nothing like that."

Scott stared at her. He wasn't sure what to say. Ever since he had collected enough information to connect Umbra to Chloe's disappearance, he had thought of them as the lowest form of life. Everything that he had seen since then had only made that feeling stronger. "I saw Billie die," Scott murmured.

Chloe's face took on a hard expression. "I wish I had seen it," she said. "Billie almost ruined an organization that had existed for untold centuries." Her grip on Scott's hand tightened. "Umbra is a very spiritual organization, Scott. We only want to be left in peace so we can study."

Scott frowned. "I don't know. It's just that—"

Chloe got up from her chair and moved closer to him. Her marvelous blue eyes captured his attention, and the waves of her blond hair spilled down around her face. "You won't believe what we've achieved, Scott. You're going to love it."

The alarm system suddenly squawked loudly. Reluctantly Scott pulled loose from Chloe and went to the nearest security screen in the hallway. "There's a motorcycle coming."

"It must be your friend Harley," Chloe said from the kitchen.

Scott shook his head. "Harley used to have a motorcycle, but she lost it. I don't know who this is." He watched the monitor as the bike grew closer. The outside security cameras were equipped with low-light sensors, but he was unable to make out anything of the motorcycle's rider but his dark clothes and helmet. Scott was considering going for a weapon again when he recognized the rider on the back. "It's Dee!" he exclaimed. "The guy in the front must be Kenyon."

Chloe got up from her seat in the kitchen and joined him at the screen. "I'm glad they're here. Now you can tell them what's going on, and we can leave."

Scott nodded slowly. "Yeah, I guess."

The motorcycle halted in the circular drive. A moment

later the front door burst open. Kenyon came in shouting. "Scott!" he bellowed. "Where are you?"

"I'm right here," Scott replied. He stepped into the foyer to meet Kenyon. "And I've got news. I found—"

Kenyon waved a gloved hand. "Save it," he said. "Harley's missing. Dee thinks she's been kidnapped."

Dee came hurrying in through the door. "We need your big brain detector," she said. "That's the only way we can find . . ." Dee's words trailed away, and her eyes widened. She raised a hand and pointed over Scott's shoulder. "Who is *that?*"

Chloe slipped around Scott and walked toward Dee with her hand outstretched. "I'm Chloe Adair," she said. "And you must be Dee."

Dee looked Chloe up and down. "Yeah, I sort of have to be Dee," she said. "But you can't possibly be *the* Chloe?" She held her hand up at shoulder level. "Chloe is supposed to be Scott's lost little sister."

Chloe laughed. "That was a long time ago," she said. "And I'm not really his sister."

"I see." Dee looked over at Scott with an expression in her eyes that could have burned through lead plates. "How wonderful that you found her, Scott. Tell me, just *how* did you find her?"

"Um, I . . . I . . . ," Scott stuttered.

It was Chloe who provided the answer. "I found him, actually. And just in time." She moved back to Scott and slipped her arm around his waist. "Scott's in terrible danger."

"Oh yeah," Dee said. "I'll agree with that."

Kenyon stepped into the middle of the hallway. "Look," he said. "It's great that he found you. We'll have a big celebration later and eat cake till we all get sick, but right now we need to find Harley."

"Right." Scott nodded, glad to have something to distract him from the situation with Dee. "Do you have any idea who took her?"

"Not really," said Dee, her eyes still on Chloe. "Abel told me someone was going after Harley. By the time I got to the beach house, she was already gone."

"Who's Abel?" asked Scott.

Kenyon walked to the security console and flipped through the cameras. "Dee was contacted by someone who claims to be from the same organization as Agent Cain. She may be lying, but Harley is gone." He stopped and backed up, then he turned toward Scott. "Three of the cameras and half a dozen sensors are off-line. What's been going on here?"

With Chloe's unexpected appearance, Scott had almost forgotten about explaining his earlier visit from Rhinehardt. "It was Legion," he said.

"*Legion* was here?" asked Kenyon. "What were they doing here?"

Chloe stepped closer to Kenyon. "They were looking for me," she said. "They want to take me back and use me in one of their awful experiments. They want to use Scott, too."

Kenyon looked at Chloe for a moment, then turned toward Scott. "Is that right?"

"Yeah," said Scott. "I guess so." He knew he

161

should explain to Kenyon how he had invited the Legion agent into the house, but Chloe's version of the story was much simpler, and Kenyon did seem to be in a hurry.

"All right," said Kenyon. "We'll have to sort this out and improve the security systems when we get back. But first we have to go find Harley. Where's the detector?"

"It's upstairs," said Scott. "In the computer room."

Kenyon ran to the end of the hallway and started up the stairs two at a time. Dee stayed where she was near the door, staring at Chloe. "Why is Legion after you?"

Chloe shook her head. "They say I'm part of their big program."

"Really," said Dee. She nodded slowly. "So they've been cooking you for two thousand years." She looked Chloe up and down again. "I guess they know what they're doing."

Kenyon came charging back down the stairs. He had the detector in one hand, a pistol in the other, and a rifle strapped across his back. "All right," he said. "We're ready to go." He held out the pistol to Scott. "You take this and follow in the car. I'll ride out front."

"Scott can't go with you," Chloe said softly.

Kenyon turned toward her with a scowl. "What do you mean?"

Chloe didn't seem to be intimidated by Kenyon's harsh expression. She took hold of Scott's hand. "Legion will be coming back very soon, and they'll

162

be able to detect me from miles away. I have to leave."

"And Scott is going with you," added Dee.

"Yes." Chloe nodded. "Scott and I have been apart so long, we can't risk being separated now."

Kenyon looked back at Scott. "What do you say?"

"I don't know," said Scott. "I mean, I want to help Harley, but—" He stopped and shrugged. "I'm no shooter, Kenyon. I won't be much use to you in a fight. Besides . . ."

"You want to be with Chloe." Kenyon stared at him for a moment longer, then nodded. "All right, good luck to you." Without a word of good-bye he turned and started toward the door. "Come on, Dee. We've got a job to do." Loaded with guns and the detector, he stepped out into the night.

Scott pulled free of Chloe's hand and walked over to Dee. "Dee, I'm sorry. I didn't want it to be like this."

There was a brightness in Dee's eyes. "I always worried that you spent too much time looking for Chloe," she said. "I guess I *really* should have worried about you *finding* her."

"Dee—"

Dee shook her head. "No," she said. "You go on with Chloe." Her lips turned up in a shadow of Dee's usual smile. "I guess I never was meant to have a date for the spring dance." She stepped forward and planted a quick kiss on Scott's cheek, then she spun around and hurried after Kenyon.

Scott stood frozen in the doorway. His emotions

were so tangled, he didn't know where to start unraveling them. In one day he had experienced more pain and more joy than he had known in five years.

Chloe stepped up at his side and put her hand lightly on his arm. "We should go," she said softly. "Are you ready?"

Scott nodded slowly. "I can't think of any reason for me to stay."

THIRTEEN

Harley floated in the yellow fluid.

Through the thick liquid and the glass tube she saw a twisted, distorted view of the room beyond. But she could hear nothing, feel nothing, sense nothing of her own body. She knew that she must be drawing the fluid into her lungs and breathing it like some terrible liquid air, but she couldn't feel her lungs at work or hear her heart beating. Even her blinking was out of her control.

The warped form of Agent Morris appeared at the door of the room. He walked over to the tube and smiled at her through the glass, then he turned a knob on the console.

Do you hear me, Ms. Davisidaro?

The voice sounded through Harley's head with such force that she wanted to scream. But of course, she couldn't scream. She could no more use her voice than she could any other part of her paralyzed, useless body.

Don't try to answer with your voice. Answer with your mind.

Harley tried. I hear you, she thought.

Louder, Ms. Davisidaro. I'm having a hard time picking you up.

I hear you.

Louder.

Harley discovered that even without a body, you can still feel pain. The powerful, demanding voice in her mind brought with it a searing agony that had no match in the physical world. *I hear you,* she thought furiously. *I hear you already. Now shut up.*

Dry laughter sounded through her mind. * *Very good. You're progressing quite well.* *

What are you doing to me?

* *I thought that would be obvious,* * replied the voice in her head. * *We're preparing you to power the sphere.* * Through the tube Harley saw Morris bend down and consult some instrument amid the tangled mass of machinery. * *Your output is already up by thirty percent.* *

Harley tried to glare at him through the tube. She wished she had at least enough control to show how she felt about the man by the expression on her face. *I'll never power your sphere. You might as well let me loose.*

Morris smiled again. * *That's one of the wonderful things about the fluid you're living in. Soon you won't have anything to say about what you will or won't do. The fluid has already removed your control over your body. In a matter of hours it will remove your control of your mind.* *

For a moment Harley didn't respond. She guarded her thoughts, keeping them below the level where the false NSA agent could hear. She remembered when she had seen the woman in a tube like this—the woman who was almost certainly her mother. When she had looked into the woman's eyes, there had been some vital spark missing.

Ever since she found her father's journals, Harley

had feared that her mother had been damaged in an experiment created by her father. But no matter what secrets he had held from her, Harley knew her father would never have put his wife into such a device and drowned her in this paralyzing soup. What had been done to her mother had been done by Unit 17, by Morris and other men like him.

* I'm going to go and prepare the chamber, * Morris sent. * In a few hours we'll be back to collect you. Of course, you'll be completely insane by then, but such is the price of getting what we need. *

This time Harley made no efforts to hide her thoughts. When I get out of here, I'm going to kill you.

* Might be frightened, * Morris replied. * But you're never getting out. * He smiled through the glass and waggled his fingers in a cheerful wave, then he strolled confidently from the room.

167

FOURTEEN

"Turn left," Dee called over the radio. "The signal is definitely coming from the west."

She watched through the windshield as Kenyon leaned the bike into a left-hand turn down a narrow road. He was obviously no expert rider—the turn was a little wobbly—but he cut a good figure on the bike. Between the black leather jacket and the rifle strapped across his back, he looked like a recruitment poster for a new sequel of *Terminator*.

Dee turned the van onto the road behind Kenyon. She glanced down at the detector on the seat beside her. The light on the screen was brighter. With one hand on the wheel Dee reached over and adjusted the knob, then she picked up the microphone and pressed the button. "All right," she called. "It looks like we're about a half mile out."

"Okay," Kenyon replied. His voice cracked and popped over the radio. "Keep a lookout for security measures."

"Right." Dee hung the radio mike back on its rack.

She was glad that the van radio didn't transmit constantly like the unit inside the motorcycle helmet. If it had, then Kenyon would have been treated to quite a chorus of sniffling, sobbing, and cursing on their drive. So far she had been able to contain her feelings about

Scott long enough to put on a good radio voice, but Dee couldn't keep her feelings from eating at her gut like acid.

Scott was the first guy she had gotten close to in years, and she had felt more for him than she ever had for any of the students from Stone Harbor. She had thought she really knew Scott. She thought their relationship was moving toward something really serious. She thought he loved her. "Well, I guess you called that wrong," she accused herself aloud in the empty van.

The brake light flared on the motorcycle, and Dee saw Kenyon slow to a stop. She picked up the microphone. "What's wrong?"

"There's a gate across the road," he called back. There was nothing but static for a few seconds, then Kenyon spoke again. "It looks like an automatic gate, and I don't see anyone around. I'm going to get a closer look."

Dee kept her distance behind him as he went up to the gate. "What's it look like up there?"

"The gate's nothing but a bar," Kenyon replied. Dee watched as Kenyon got off the motorcycle, leaned it sharply to the side, and walked it under the gate.

"What about me?" Dee asked. "How do we handle the van?"

"There are two choices: around or through."

Dee looked at the side of the road. There were ditches on either side with water standing in them and clusters of stunted trees lining the road. "Get out of the way," she called. She waited until Kenyon had ridden the bike another hundred yards down the narrow road, then she checked her seat belt, gripped the wheel, and hit the gas.

The big van rang like a bell when it hit the gate, and Dee was jerked hard against her shoulder straps, but the gate definitely came off worse in the collision. It snapped off and went flying into the bushes.

Dee skidded to a stop and climbed out of the van. The impact of the gate had knocked a dent almost six inches deep into the front of the vehicle, and a thin stream of steam jetted from under the hood, but it looked to her like the van would operate for a few more miles. She climbed back in and gave Kenyon the signal to continue.

They traveled for no more than a minute before the top of a building appeared above the trees. It was a new building with a front of dark, smoked glass and burnished steel. It rose a good four stories above a wide, sparsely populated parking lot. The building was absolutely free of identifying markings. No signs, no street numbers, nothing.

Kenyon stopped the motorcycle at the edge of the parking lot, and Dee pulled up beside him. "What now?" she asked.

Kenyon got off the bike, removed his helmet, and hung it from the handlebars. "What does the detector say?"

Dee checked the reading. "As far as I can tell, it says she's in there." She picked up the little box and thumped it on the side. "This thing is acting strange. It shows the power level going up, and it's getting kind of erratic."

"Maybe something is happening to Harley," said Kenyon. He unstrapped the rifle from his back and laid it across the seat of the motorcycle. "We should move in quickly."

Dee climbed out of the van, stretched, and surveyed the office building. "Who do you think is behind this one?" she asked. "Unit 17? Legion?"

Kenyon shrugged. "Does it matter? All we have to do is go in there and get Harley out."

"Right." Dee looked at the entrance. The lower level of the building was mostly metal. It looked cool from a distance, but there were no windows big enough to drive a van through. She was willing to bet that was a carefully thought-out part of the design. "Okay," she said. "Why don't I go up front and walk into the lobby? I'll talk to the receptionist. I'll pretend to be, oh, a lost tourist or something. Then, while I'm drawing attention, you can . . . you can . . . Kenyon? Are you listening to me?"

In the middle of her speech Kenyon had walked around to the rear of the van. "I'm listening," he said. He pulled open the van's back doors. "Go ahead. What do you want me to do?"

"Right," Dee continued. "When I'm inside, you ride around back and see if there's anything like a loading bay or a service entrance, and then—" She stopped again.

Kenyon had pulled something that looked like a green metal suitcase from the van and laid it down on the blacktop parking lot. He opened it to reveal a black tube about three feet long and a trio of things that looked like dull green traffic cones.

"What is that thing?" asked Dee.

Kenyon picked up one of the cones and snapped it neatly onto the end of the tube. "Can you tell where Harley is in that building?"

"Near the back," Dee replied. "Why?"

"Go on with your story," Kenyon said. "After we find the service entrance, we take the van around and . . ."

Dee heard a loud whoosh of air as the green cone leaped off the end of the tube on a tongue of flame. The cone zipped past Dee, arced over the rows of cars near the building, and smacked into the metal front. A moment later an enormous, stomach-kicking explosion shook the ground.

Shattered glass sprayed out across the parking lot and twisted chunks of metal rained onto the blacktop. A cloud of dust and fire rose up into the sky in a miniature mushroom cloud.

"What were you saying?" asked Kenyon.

Dee shook her head to try and clear her ringing ears. "I was just saying, 'or we could blow the front of the building off.'" She pointed at the tube in Kenyon's hand. "What *is* that thing?"

"Russian RVG-7 antitank weapon."

Kenyon bent down, picked up a second cone, and snapped it into place.

As she watched him load the weapon Dee was struck by a strange idea. He loves her, she thought. Kenyon would do anything for Harley. Dee wasn't sure anyone had ever loved her that much. She had thought Scott loved her, but it was clear now that she had been mistaken. "You know," she began. "Harley is—"

Kenyon looked at her sharply. "What about Harley?"

She's lucky to have you. "Nothing," said Dee. "Let's just get her out of this place."

"That's the plan," said Kenyon. He held the missile launcher in one hand, reached for the gun sitting on the motorcycle, and tossed it to Dee. "Keep alert," he said. "I expect them to come for us now."

"Yeah, if there are any of them left." Dee peered at the gun she was holding. It was the sleekest, blackest, meanest-looking gun she had ever seen, and it was utterly strange. "All right," she said. "And what is this one?"

"South African Striker antiriot shotgun," Kenyon replied. "It fires a dozen twelve-gauge shells in just over two seconds. If they come, just point it and squeeze the trigger. But be careful—it kicks."

"Uh-huh," said Dee. "I'll just bet it does." She held up the jet black weapon and sighted along the barrel. "Why do I get the feeling you haven't been buying this stuff at the local sporting goods store?"

Before Kenyon could say anything more, a warbling siren split the air. From around the side of the building a long black car approached. A man was leaning out the passenger-side window. Dee heard a buzzing noise, like a circular saw gone mad, and the pavement near her feet suddenly flew into the air. It wasn't until it happened a second time that Dee realized they were being shot at.

The second cone roared away from the end of the launcher. It missed the car, striking the blacktop a half-dozen feet to the left. It didn't matter. The force of the exploding shell flung the car into the air. It came down on its roof twenty feet away, smashed into another car, and began to burn. There was no more shooting.

Another car appeared. This time Kenyon's shot was more accurate. The antitank weapon split the sedan like a can opener, leaving metal fragments the size of a thumbnail scattered over a hundred-foot circle.

"That's it for me," said Kenyon. He tossed the launcher onto the ground.

"What do we do with the next one?" asked Dee.

Kenyon gestured at the gun in her hands. "The next one is all yours."

"Great."

But no more cars pulled out from behind the building. Dee and Kenyon stood at the edge of the parking lot waiting for at least five minutes, and no other enemies appeared.

Kenyon shook his head. "I don't like this," he said. "It's too easy."

Dee shrugged. "We could blow up some more stuff," she suggested. "Maybe that will get them *really* angry."

Kenyon shot her a withering look. "Let's just go in and get Harley."

Dee collected the detector while Kenyon swapped his empty rocket launcher for another source of destruction. This time it was a sharp-angled gun that looked like Darth Vader's hunting rifle. Dee didn't bother to ask what it was called. Together they advanced between the rows of cars toward the smoking building. All the way across the parking lot Dee expected someone to open up on them with a machine gun, or a death ray, or a flock of screaming mutant bats, but they reached the edge of the rubble without incident.

She looked at the smoldering debris and shook her head. "I sure hope this doesn't turn out to be an IRS office," she said. "Or we are going to be in *serious* trouble."

"You saw the weapon that man was firing," said Kenyon. "This is not the IRS." He waved a hand at the smoke and squinted through the ruined lobby. "These guys are Unit 17."

"That's good. I guess." Dee looked down at the detector screen. "Harley's straight ahead."

They waded across the rubble of the building's front and into a smoking cave that had been a hallway. At one point Dee saw a hand jutting from under a pile of jagged steel fragments. She tried very hard not to look.

In the hallway a woman in a white lab coat sat on the floor. There was a stunned expression on her face and a smear of blood on her forehead, but Dee was relieved to see that the woman was still alive.

The woman looked up at them and blinked. "You're here for her, aren't you?"

Kenyon turned to her and leveled the huge barrel of his gun at her chest. "Do you know where Harley is?"

175

"I know," said the woman. Her lips twitched and formed a weak smile. "I know it's too late."

"You better hope you're wrong about that," Kenyon said in a voice as cold as the grave. "If it's too late for Harley, then nothing on earth will save the rest of you."

Dee stepped around Kenyon. "Over here!" she called. The display on the detector had grown so bright that no amount of adjustment would dim the brilliant circle at the point of the screen. "I think she's in here." She tried the doorknob, and it opened smoothly.

Inside, Dee saw a mass of equipment grouped around something that looked like a big, cylindrical aquarium. The hunk of equipment was a lumpy mass of metal studded with knobs, dials, and little growths that looked much like silver mushrooms. Dee circled to the left and looked behind the machine.

"I don't understand it," she said. "The detector says she's right here, but I don't see . . ." Dee's voice trailed away because at that moment she did see. She saw what was inside the tube. "Kenyon! Get in here!"

Kenyon came running into the room. Dee heard the gun clatter from his hands, and a moment later he was standing with his palms and face pressed against the glass tube. "Harley! Harley, can you hear me?"

The thin figure inside the cylinder blinked but gave no other sign of life. "Hold on!" Kenyon shouted. "We're going to get you out of there!"

Dee circled the tube. It was easily ten feet tall and three feet across. She could see no seams. "Exactly *how* do we get her out of there?"

Kenyon shook his head. "I don't know." He put his foot on one of the metal mushrooms and climbed up onto the machine. "I think I can get the top off," he said. "But I don't know if I can pull her out if I do."

"Is this thing bolted down?" asked Dee.

"What?"

Dee lay down in the space between the floor and the wall and pushed against the base of the cylinder with her feet. It shifted only a fraction of an inch before rocking back, but it moved. "If you help me," she said, "I think we can make the top the side."

Kenyon joined her on the floor and put his feet higher on the tube. Together they began to rock the cylinder. The heavy tube jostled more with every swing, and a trickle of yellow fluid spilled out from under the lid. Inside the cylinder Harley's body swayed.

Dee grunted with the effort as the tube moved back and forth. "You think it'll hurt her if we take her out?" she asked between breaths.

"I don't think it's helping her any to be in there," Kenyon said. "I'll risk taking her out."

The cylinder came close to toppling on the next swing, then fell back hard. Dee nearly screamed as the tube loomed over her for a moment, then it rocked to the side and fell to the floor with an earsplitting crash.

Whatever the tube was made from, it obviously wasn't glass. The fall didn't so much as crack it. But as Kenyon had predicted, the top of the cylinder popped loose on impact. A gusher of yellow fluid spilled out onto the floor, and with it slid the limp form of Harley Davisidaro.

Kenyon scrambled to her side. "Harley!" He grabbed her under the arms and eased her into a sitting position. "Harley, are you okay?"

Yellow fluid poured from Harley's mouth. Dee watched as her friend's chest jerked in, out, then froze.

"Do something!" she cried. "She's not breathing!"

Kenyon looked up with helpless eyes. "I don't know CPR," he said desperately. "Do you?"

"Not really." Dee crouched in the yellow puddle beside Harley. "Breathe!" she shouted into her face. "C'mon, Harley, *breathe!*"

Harley didn't breathe. Her dark eyes blinked again, then began to slowly close.

Dee threw her shotgun onto the floor and shoved Kenyon out of the way. "Move!" She got around behind Harley and lifted her body from the floor. Harley's long legs dragged across the tile, but Dee held her chest up, balled her hands together into fists, and shoved them under Harley's ribs. She shoved up and in as hard as she could.

Fluid spilled from Harley's mouth, and her head dropped to the side. She didn't breathe.

Dee drew in a deep breath of her own and tried again. She braced herself and squeezed as if she meant to press her fists right through Harley.

An explosion of fluid sprayed from Harley's mouth. Then, to Dee's immense relief, Harley drew in a great, whistling breath. Dee staggered. "Okay," she said. "You can take her now."

Kenyon got an arm under Harley's long legs, another

behind her head, and lifted her. He held her fluid-soaked body against himself with a mixture of determination and tenderness. "Come on," he said. "Let's get out of here."

"I'm afraid I can't allow that," a voice declared from the door. A man with gray hair and a dark suit stepped into the room. Dee saw her shotgun lying on the wet floor and hurried toward it, but the man put his foot on top of the gun. He produced a strange, boxy-looking pistol and directed it toward Dee. "Can't let you have that," he said. He gestured with the gun. "Go over there, please, beside your friends."

Muscles bulged along Kenyon's jaw as he grit his teeth. "You better let us go."

The man laughed. "Or *what*, Mr. Moor?" He reached into his pocket with his free hand and pulled out a cigarette. Then he extracted a lighter and began to smoke. "I've been trying to cut down on these," he said. "But this seems like an excellent time for a smoke."

"Hey, don't stop on my account," said Dee. "You seem like a great candidate for lung cancer."

The man smiled around his cigarette. "Very funny. I'm afraid I don't know your name, young lady. And at this stage there's not much point in introducing yourself." He waved the gun toward Kenyon. "In one way you've made this very simple," he said. He drew the cigarette from his mouth and blew out a stream of blue-white smoke.

Dee felt a weight tugging against her. She reached into her windbreaker and found the smooth metal curves of her father's old police revolver.

"You see," said the smoking man, "we were given two options in this operation. We could recruit Ms. Davisidaro. . . ." He smiled again. "Or we could simply kill you all." With that the man raised the gun and pointed it toward Kenyon.

Kenyon shook his head. "This isn't over."

"Oh, but I believe it is," replied the man.

Dee drew out her father's gun, pointed it at the man, and fired. And fired. And fired. And fired. She pressed the trigger until no sound came out but the dry click of the hammer striking an empty cylinder.

The man in the black suit seemed to have acquired a new set of buttons. Only these buttons oozed a thick green liquid onto the cloth of his suit. The look on his face changed from smug confidence to an expression of utter disbelief. The cigarette fell from his lips and hissed as it struck the fluid covering the floor. The man took one step back, then collapsed in a heap.

Dee stared down at the dead man. "I killed him," she whispered.

Still holding Harley in his arms, Kenyon struggled toward the door. "Come on!" he exclaimed. "Let's get out of here before anyone else shows up."

But Dee couldn't take her eyes off the broken form on the floor. "I killed him," she repeated. "I killed him."

Kenyon walked back across the floor and put his face close to Dee's. "You killed him," he said. "And good for you. Because if you hadn't, it would be us lying on the floor. Now, are you ready to go?"

The revolver slipped from Dee's fingers and

bounced beside the dead man's head. Dee nodded quickly. "Yeah," she answered. "Very, very ready."

"Then let's get out of here."

It took longer to walk back to the van. Kenyon was burdened with carrying Harley, and they were both well coated with the yellow fluid, which made their footing slippery. By the time they reached the vehicles, Dee had stopped trembling, though the image of the dead man was still waiting for her every time she closed her eyes.

Dee jerked open the sliding door at the side of the van, and Kenyon lifted Harley inside. "Hold on," he whispered to her gently. "We're taking you home." Harley slumped in her seat, limp as a wet rag.

Dee ran around to the driver's side and started to crank the engine, but when she looked in the rearview mirror, she stopped. "Kenyon!" she shouted. "It looks like the evil marines are on their way!"

Along the single-lane road leading to the office building a line of vehicles was moving slowly forward. The ones in front seemed to be normal cars, but behind those Dee could see other shapes that appeared to be armored vehicles and possibly even tanks.

"How are we going to get out of here?" she asked.

Kenyon stood beside the van and surveyed the approaching convoy of Unit 17 vehicles. "The motorcycle," he declared. "We'll get out through the woods."

"You can't put three people on a motorcycle," said Dee.

"Want to bet?" Kenyon reached into the van and pulled Harley out again. "Have you ever driven a motorcycle?"

Dee shrugged. "Once or twice. My cousin has one."

"Good," said Kenyon. "You're our driver. Get on and slide forward as far as you can."

Dee had her doubts about the plan, but there was no time to argue. Already the first of the slow-moving cars was nearing the edge of the parking lot.

Kenyon put Harley on the bike behind Dee and draped her limp arms over Dee's shoulders. "Hold on to her for a second—I've got to do something before we can go."

"It better be fast," said Dee.

She looked back and watched as Kenyon dragged a second case from the back of the van. This one opened to reveal a simple gray box topped with a cluster of buttons. Kenyon consulted a scrap of paper and began tapping quickly on the small keypad.

"What is that?" Dee asked. "A nuclear bomb?"

Kenyon pressed a final button, then ran toward the bike. He slid on the back, pressing Dee so far forward that she was sitting on the gas tank instead of the seat. He reached around Harley and got his hands up as far as Dee's sides. "Okay," he said. "Now go!"

"Which way?"

"Into the woods," Kenyon replied. "Any direction you want but away from here."

Dee started the bike and rolled across the parking lot. It took her a few seconds to get the feel of the big machine, especially with the weight of the extra riders. But by the time she reached the edge of the blacktop, she was starting to get the hang of it.

The buzz saw whine of a Unit 17 gun sounded, and a tree beside them was split in half by a cluster of hypersonic metal scraps. Dee squeezed the handle and flew into the woods.

"What do I do if we come to a fence?" she asked.

Kenyon leaned forward and shouted to be heard over the wind and the motorcycle. "You better hope there *isn't* a fence."

"Why?"

"Because we've got less than thirty seconds before that box goes off."

Dee twisted the throttle again. Pine needles sprayed from the bike's rear wheel in a brown wake, and vines slapped against her face, but she didn't let off the gas.

Thirty seconds later Dee saw the sky behind them turn white in the motorcycle's rearview mirror. The flash was followed by a mound of fire rising to the sky. Carried on the crest of the explosion, trees, vehicles, and fragments of building tumbled like matchsticks caught in a wave. The sound arrived a few moments later. It was almost too deep to call it a sound—a bass rumbled that literally shook Dee's bones, rattled her teeth, and made it hard to control the motorcycle.

Right on the heels of the noise came a blast of scorching wind that left Dee gasping for air. Behind them the fireball mounted higher and higher into the sky.

Dee smiled grimly. They'd made it.

"Wow," said a slurred voice at Dee's shoulder.

Dee turned her head slightly. "Harley, was that you?"

Harley nodded and mumbled something.

"What?"

"Great exit," said Harley.

EPILOGUE

Harley Davisidaro savored the sensation of being dry. Even if her clothing was one of Kenyon's T-shirts and a pair of gym shorts that were three sizes too big, at least they were dry clothes. She thought she might just skip a bath for a week or two.

She stumbled down the stairs in time to see Dee get off the phone. "Was your father mad?"

"He's on his way out here," said Dee. "I'm not sure he's exactly mad."

"Well, that's good," said Harley.

"He's not exactly mad," Dee repeated. "It's more like the white-hot fury generated by a thousand colliding galaxies."

"Oh," said Harley. "Sorry."

The front door of the mansion opened, and Kenyon came in. "There's something outside that I want you two to see," he said.

"What is it?" asked Harley.

"It's better if you see."

Kenyon led the way around the big house. "I was checking the burned-out security cameras on the perimeter," he said as he walked. "It looked like there had been some kind of power overload, but I didn't find anything really odd until I came to this." He pointed to the ground.

Harley peered down. "This" turned out to be the body of a middle-aged man with pinched features and

184

thinning hair. From the size of the hole in the man's chest, there was no doubt he was dead. "Who is he?"

Kenyon shook his head. "I don't know for sure, but he was carrying these papers." He held up a thin packet of sheets. "As near as I can figure out, these are a series of communications between a part of Unit 17 and a part of Umbra."

Harley frowned. "Why would Umbra and Unit 17 be talking? I thought they were enemies."

"Anything you can make sense of?" asked Dee.

"Yeah." Kenyon flipped through the pages. "They may be enemies, but it seems there are some things they can agree on." He pulled a sheet from the middle of the packet and held it out to Harley. "This is a communication from Umbra offering to turn over your false ID and probable location."

"That explains the poster and requests that came through my father's office," said Dee. "Umbra was telling them where to look, and they had your new name from that FBI thing back in D.C."

Harley gave a tired laugh. "Wonderful. These guys are at war forever, and the only thing they agree on is that they both want me dead. Is there anything else in those papers?"

Kenyon shrugged. "Most of the rest means nothing to me, but there is one very interesting point."

"What's that?"

"The sender." Kenyon tapped the final sheet. "The offer to sell out Harley came from one Chloe Adair."

To be continued . . .

What's it like to be a Witch?

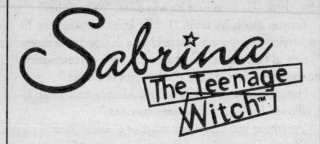

Sabrina
The Teenage Witch™

"I'm 16, I'm a Witch, and I *still* have to go to school?"

◆◆◆◆◆

#1 Sabrina, the Teenage Witch
by David Cody Weiss and Bobbi JG Weiss

#2 Showdown at the Mall
by Diana G. Gallagher

#3 Good Switch, Bad Switch
by David Cody Weiss and Bobbi JG Weiss

#4 Halloween Havoc
by Diana Gallagher

#5 Santa's Little Helper
by Cathy East Dubowski

Based on the hit TV series

Look for a new title every other month.

From Archway Paperbacks
Published by Pocket Books

1345-04

ARCHWAY PAPERBACKS

EXTREME ZONE #7

PROOF OF PURCHASE OFFER

OFFICIAL RULES

1. To receive your free EXTREME ZONE baseball cap (approximate retail value: $8.00), submit this completed Official Entry Form and at least one Official Entry Form from either books 1, 2, 3, 4, 5, or 6 (no copies allowed). Offer good only while supplies last. Allow 6-8 weeks for delivery. Send entries to the Archway Paperbacks/EZ Promotion, 13th Floor, 1230 Avenue of the Americas, NY, NY 10020.

2. The offer is open to residents of the U.S. and Canada. Void where prohibited. Employees of Simon & Schuster, Inc., its parent, subsidiaries, suppliers, affiliates, agencies, participating retailers, and their families living in the same household are not eligible. One EXTREME ZONE baseball cap per person. Offer expires 12/31/97.

3. Not responsible for lost, late, postage due or misdirected responses. Requests not complying with all offer requirements will not be honored. Any fraudulent submission will be prosecuted to the fullest extent permitted by law.